Akio And The Dream World

Carl A. Snook

Published by New Generation Publishing in 2015

Copyright © Carl Snook 2015

First Edition

The author asserts the moral right under the Copyright, Designs and Patents Act 1988 to be identified as the author of this work.

All Rights reserved. No part of this publication may be reproduced, stored in a retrieval system or transmitted, in any form or by any means without the prior consent of the author, nor be otherwise circulated in any form of binding or cover other than that which it is published and without a similar condition being imposed on the subsequent purchaser.

www.newgeneration-publishing.com

New Generation Publishing

Chapter 1

The New World

It is often said that when we dream, we are taken to another world where anything is possible, but the question has always remained: what if the line between dreams and reality was crossed?

Akio's father had been offered a promotion at work, which would mean that the family would be moving to the big city. Akio didn't like the idea of moving to a new place, but the upside was that the whole department was moving, so Jiro and his family were going too. Akio and Jiro had been friends for a long time. They had grown up together in the small town of Urayasu.

The two boys rode together in Akio's father's car, both waiting to find out what the city would be like and what it would have to offer. Neither one of them had ever been outside of the town before. It was going to be a completely different life for both of them.

"So. Are you two ready for the big city?" asked Akio's dad from the front of the car. "It'll be very different to the country," he added. Both boys had been relatively quiet for most of the journey. "It will be your sixteenth birthday soon Akio, we could do a big house-warming party and include your birthday, that would be good huh?"

Akio looked at his dad. "Maybe," he answered shrugging it off before going back to looking out the car window.

"Look, I know you didn't want to move, but try to see this as an adventure. You never know what might happen," his dad said trying to raise Akio's spirits.

"Not much of an adventure," Akio whispered under his breath.

Soon enough they arrived in the city. There were tall buildings, lots of people and the smell of fumes in the air. This definitely was different from the country. After driving for a little while longer, they pulled up to a cul-de-sac of houses. Jiro's parents and the moving van were waiting for them on the curb. The movers had started work on moving everything into the two houses, which stood side-by-side, almost identical. Jiro's mum was directing them on what went into which house.

"Here we are boys, home sweet home," said Akio's dad. The car pulled up and Akio and Jiro got out of the car then looked up at the two houses. They were tall, white houses with dark roofs. Akio's mouth cracked a small smile. It looked a lot bigger than his old house, with a front porch and white, wooden look to it. There was a small gap between the houses both with gates leading to the back gardens. Maybe it wouldn't be as bad as he thought.

"Here are your bags boys," said Akio's mum handing them the bags. "Go pick and sort out your rooms and then we can have some lunch later." The boys took their bags and made their way into the houses. They went into Jiro's house first and ran up the stairs. They ran around the rooms until they found one that Jiro liked.

"Mum, can I have this one?" shouted Jiro out the window to his parents.

"Yes I'm sure that's okay," his dad shouted back. He threw his bag down and then the two boys ran out of the house and next door to Akio's house. Again they ran up the stairs and checked out all the rooms. Akio decided that he liked the one to the left of the house because his window faced Jiro's. He shouted down to his dad,

"Dad, this one's window faces Jiro's."

"Okay then Akio. You can have that one," his dad shouted back. He threw down his bag and the boys decided to check out the rest of the house.

"Jiro," shouted his mum from outside. "Sorting out your room doesn't mean pick it and just through your bag down, start unpacking please."

"I have to go Akio, I'll see you tomorrow." Jiro then left and went home, so Akio went back up to his room and started emptying his bag. He opened up his closet and it was really big. The movers brought his bed up and put it together while Akio filled his draws and closet with his clothes. It didn't take the movers long so Akio asked his mum for some bed sheets and put them on the bed. For the rest of the night he sorted through boxes that the movers brought up gradually until it was time to go to bed. The day hadn't been too bad and Akio was a little happier with the situation.

The next morning, Akio came downstairs to breakfast on the table. The radio was playing in the background as his dad bit into his toast.

"Record numbers of people are falling into what doctors are calling the deep sleep. No symptoms have been shown that these are comas of any kind. The brains of these people are still showing signs of working normally. People are just not waking up. Is this through choice? More developments as they come. Now the weather," announced the man on the radio. Akio's dad looked up and noticed Akio standing in the kitchen doorway.

"Morning champ, how was the sleep?" he asked. Akio wandered into the kitchen and sat down opposite his dad.

"Pretty good, thanks dad," replied Akio.

"What's the plan for your day then son? What sort of adventure waits?" asked Akio's dad. "Why don't you and Jiro jump on the bus to the city centre, check it out?"

"That sound's good. I'll go and get changed and then go round to get him," said Akio standing up. He then jogged upstairs, but paused as he saw something fly past the window. It had looked like a train track in the sky. He dismissed the idea, as it sounded crazy; a train in the sky? He then continued on to his room.

A few minutes later he came out and downstairs, dressed ready to go out.

"I'll see you later then," Shouted Akio towards the kitchen as he went through the front door.

"Okay son," his dad shouted back with his mouth full.

Akio ran outside and stepped up to Jiro's front door. Just as he was about to knock on the door he heard someone shout his name. He looked over and saw Jiro coming through the garden gate.

"Hi Akio," Said Jiro.

"Hi Jiro, I was thinking we could get on a bus and go check out the city centre or something, my dad thinks we could have some kind of adventure, although I don't suspect it will be that exciting. You want to?" asked Akio.

"Yeah sure, let me just tell my parents and I'll be ready," replied Jiro who then ran inside as Akio waited on the porch. A minute later Jiro returned outside.

"Ready to go?" he asked.

"Yeah let's go," said Akio. They both then left Jiro's porch and headed down the road towards the bus stop at the end. As they were walking a bus drove past them.

"Quickly," said Akio. The boys started to run towards the bus stop, but as they reached it, the bus closed its doors and started to pull away. They both sighed and Jiro went over to the bus timetable that was up on the post.

"There isn't going to be a bus for an hour now," he said. "Maybe we should head back and come back later?" he asked.

"Maybe," said Akio.

"You don't want to? It will be boring waiting here," asked Jiro. "I'm going back," he said and then started to walk away.

"We could just wait, one might turn up." Akio shouted as Jiro was turning the corner. But Jiro didn't hear and turned the corner. Akio sat down on the curb. He didn't want to go back to the house and do nothing. He wanted to at least try to have an adventure like his dad had said.

Seconds later Akio heard a sound of an engine approaching. He looked up and saw a bus.

"That's funny." Akio whispered to himself. How come one had come so quickly? The bus was an older-looking bus with dark windows and a rusty colour to it. It stopped in front of him and the door opened. Akio looked up into the bus; it looked as old inside as it did on the outside. The driver's window was closed with just a sign saying: No Charge, Please take a seat. Akio looked up the road to the corner. Jiro obviously wasn't going to come back, and this might be the only bus for an hour. He thought for a second before stepping up into the bus. All the seats were empty so Akio walked down to the back and sat down. The door closed and the bus pulled away.

"Sir, is this going to the city centre?" shouted Akio down the bus. But the driver gave no answer, just a hand with thumbs up that came from the drivers cab. He went to try and look out the window, but the windows were too blackened out to see much and he didn't want to get his hand dirty, so he just sat back in the seat. There was a mechanical destination wheel on the roof of the bus that at that moment rolled round to a sign that said Two minutes. Shouldn't it say a place rather than a time? And how would it get there so quickly? Everything about this didn't seem normal.

After those two minutes, exactly on the dot, the bus stopped and opened its doors. The hand reappeared from the driver's cab holding a map. Akio got up cautiously and walked over to the hand.

"Thank you," said Akio as he took the map. Just as he was about to step off the bus, a voice came from the cab that said, "Don't let your mind become clear. Remember, or the map is useless." Akio got off the bus and the doors then shut. It then spluttered and banged before heading off. Akio looked around, but only saw a train station. He was not in the neighborhood anymore, nor was he in the city centre. He looked at the map. It was almost completely blank except for the train station in the bottom right-hand corner. It seemed the only option was to catch a train, as he couldn't see another bus timetable. If he was going to have an adventure he couldn't just give up and turn back anyway, so he carried on.

Akio walked up the stone stairs and up onto a short wooden platform. He looked up the track. It was an unusual track that looked like it bent upwards the further it went on. Akio squinted to see how far up it went. He couldn't see, but would find out once he was on the train. This must be what he had seen the day before. He knew he had really seen it, but it couldn't be possible, could it?

No one seemed to be around except Akio and the people who drove the transports. There was a bench over by the metal fence, so Akio went and sat down. He couldn't understand why the map was so empty, and what had the driver meant about remembering? A map isn't much use if there's nothing on it. After a while an old train pulled up to the station and Akio got on. Why was everything so old? Again, there was no one else on the train, but he wanted to see where the tracks lead.

"Weird," muttered Akio. He sat down and the train started and proceeded up the track. He knelt up on the seats and looked out the windows. The track went higher and higher, and the train went faster and faster, until it shot through the clouds. Akio clenched tightly onto the seat. The sunlight was beaming through the windows as he looked on in wonderment.

The train glided over clouds with birds whooshing past, and in the distance there was a city in the sky. Akio couldn't believe what he was experiencing, what he was seeing. The train raced towards the city, clouds flying past the windows. As the train approached the station it started to slow. It came to a stop and the doors slid open. Akio let go of the seat and stepped off the train and onto the wooden platform. Again no one was about, but he saw a path leading away from the station. He walked up the path to two big silver gates. There, standing on a shining podium, was man in a white and silver suit waiting by the gates.

"Your name, young sir?" asked the man.

"My name? My name is Akio," He replied. The man took his eyes away from the clipboard and looked at Akio. He smiled and said, "Welcome to Skye City."

The gates began to open to reveal a magnificent market walk, with people everywhere, laughing with each other, having conversations and selling all kinds of things from their stalls. Akio stood there with his jaw dropped, motionless.

"Go in young sir, it's okay," said the man at the gate. Akio looked back at him and then proceeded to walk into the city. He looked left, he looked right. What an amazing place this was. He walked up to one of the stalls.

"You, my boy!" Shouted the market stall owner. "How would you like to your very own Chika Bird? For only thirteen skillies?"

"Skillie? What's a skillie?" Asked Akio.

"Money, my boy, coins." replied the market man in his loud voice.

"I don't have anything I'm afraid," said Akio.

"I'll tell you what my boy. I like you. You're honest, a lot more honest than some of these traders, ha ha ha!" Laughed the market trader, who then bent over and picked up a box tied with twine. "Take this parcel over to the mailing room for me, four roads away, and you can take the little Chika Bird for free, how does that sound?" said the Man.

"Sure. Wow, thank you," said Akio happily taking the parcel. The Chika Bird hopped off the stand and up onto Akio's shoulder.

"Come on my little friend," said Akio to the Chika Bird. "How about I call you Tiny, would you like that? Let's get this parcel delivered yeah?" Akio and Tiny then started to head down towards the mailroom. What a nice and friendly man the market trader had been.

All along the way Akio was in wonder at the city.

"This is an amazing place, Tiny," said Akio walking down the road. All the houses down the road were old-style cottages, with huge marble buildings in the background, so tall he was blinded by the sun.

"I wonder what's in those buildings," he said to Tiny.

They reached a tall two-storey cottage, with a clock in the roof and just under a hanging sign that read "Mr. Yama's Post." Akio went in through the door and the bell sounded. Inside was a lot bigger than what you saw on the outside, with floating gloves everywhere, moving letters into pigeonholes and sorting parcels into piles. Akio walked up to a tall counter and hit the bell. Up popped a small man in glasses with electric-style white hair.

"Hello my friend, welcome to Mr. Yama's post. We've got the fastest post, down on this south coast," said the man as he dinged the bell with glee. "My name is Mr. Yama, how can I help?" Akio held up the package he was carrying over the counter.

"I have a package for you from the man at the Chika bird stand," said Akio handing it over.

"Ah yes, I've been waiting for this. Thank you young man." Mr. Yama undid the twine and pulled off the paper. Inside the parcel was what looked like a magic wand.

"What's that?" asked Akio. Mr. Yama smiled and looked down over his glasses.

"This, my boy, is a dream weaver. It is a kind of wand. So many of these letters are filled with the dreams of those who wish to share them. They send them to me so that I can read them and lift them off the page. I misplaced my old dream weaver some time ago now." Mr. Yama held it up. "And now I can continue." He grabbed a letter that was flying past. He opened the letter and tapped the paper with the wand. A light colourful picture of a man holding a fishing rod came floating off the page. He drifted it over to another envelope and placed it inside, sealing the envelope shut, and then the letter flew off into the clutches of one of the gloves.

"What happens to that now?" asked Akio watching the glove filing it away. Mr. Yama turned to face him.

"That dream will now be sent to the man it was intended for. It works for memories too."

"Wow," said Akio. "You said you're Mr. Yama right?" He asked.

"I am," replied Mr. Yama.

"I'm Akio, it's nice to meet you. But can I ask a question?"

"Certainly my boy," replied Mr. Yama.

"I don't understand how I got here. This isn't my world sir." The man stopped and looked at Akio.

"What do you mean, you don't know?" asked Mr. Yama. Akio tried to think how he could explain.

"Well, I've just moved house and I thought I'd go exploring, so I caught this bus, but it was a strange looking bus. That bus took me to a train station, and that brought me here." Mr. Yama looked troubled. He ran down from behind the counter and closed the shutters on the windows. "How old are you Akio?" Asked Mr. Yama turning around.

"I'll be sixteen soon," replied Akio. Mr. Yama looked up the ceiling and started muttering to himself. He then ran over to a ladder connected to very tall wooden shelves, knocking into the flying gloves. He climbed up very high and pulled out a very old parchment. He slid down the ladder and ran back over to Akio.

"Would your birthday happen to fall on the sixteenth?" Mr. Yama asked.

"Yes. Yes it does," Akio replied. Mr. Yama gasped and stepped backwards.

"Sixteen on sixteen," he whispered. "Do you know what this means?" he asked. "I must get you to Mrs. Fritter's inn. It's important you go there soon. We were told of this day, but were never told what it meant, nor did we think it would actually happen. If anyone can figure it out, it will be her." Mr. Yama ran over to a big sliding wooden door and wrenched it open to reveal a motor trike with a sidecar. "Hop in, Akio." Mr. Yama threw Akio a helmet and jumped on the trike himself. Akio sat in the sidecar and Mr. Yama started the engine. "Hold on, Akio," shouted Mr. Yama as he sent the trike rushing forwards out of the gates. Akio saw that Tiny was having some trouble holding on, so he took him in his hands and held him tight. They rushed down roads and past people on the street.

"What's happening?" shouted Akio to Mr. Yama. But with all the wind rushing past them, Mr. Yama didn't hear. The trike shot down a road with trees either side and came to an abrupt halt outside a white door with plants on each side. Mr. Yama knocked very hastily on the door and a few seconds later a big cherry faced woman in a flowery dress opened the door.

"Mr. Yama, what a pleasant surprise," she said.

"I'm afraid not, Mrs. Fritter." He turned to Akio. "This is Akio. On the sixteenth, he will be turning sixteen." Mrs. Fritter dropped the coffee cup she was holding in shock.

"Sixteen on sixteen," she gasped. "You must come inside." Mr. Yama walked in the door followed by Akio and Tiny. Mrs. Fritter looked around outside and then closed the door. She led them through the house and walked into a room with two settees, an armchair, a small table in the corner and a fireplace that was alight. Mrs. Fritter went to a bookcase and then re-joined them with a big black book. "Sit down, my lovelies," said Mrs. Fritter, squeezing herself into the armchair. Akio and Mr. Yama sat themselves down of one of the settee's "Now," she said opening the book. "Let's see if we can work this out then." Mr. Yama took out the dream weaver and tapped the page of the book. Out of the book came a stream of light, which he placed inside an envelope. He handed it to Mrs. Fritter who quoted the phrase "Kama Laroo." She then threw the envelope into the fire. The fire turned blue and then died down to a small flame. Inside the fire appeared a picture. It showed a man in a dark shadowed hood, holding a crystal in his hand. It then showed a land in ruin with the man kneeling in the rain. Bodies lay around and the sky was black. The picture then flew out from the fire back into the book. Words appeared on the page and Mrs. Fritter leant in to read it.

"It says," Said Mrs. Fritter. "Sixteen on sixteen. The only one who can stop dreams from ending." Mrs. Fritter looked up. "Who is he?" she asked.

"I'm not sure," replied Mr. Yama. "Whoever he is, it seems our boy Akio here is the only one who can stop him." Akio was frozen still, his face as white as the pages of the book. He then jumped to his feet and ran out of the house.

"Akio!" shouted Mr. Yama trying to stop him.

"Go after him, for goodness' sake," Mrs. Fritter yelled. Mr. Yama jumped and ran out of the house after Akio. He looked around for a while. He finally found him down the lane sitting on a bench at a pond holding Tiny in his hand. He went up and sat next to Akio on the bench.

"I can't go back can I," asked Akio with a quiver in his voice.

"I don't think so, no. Not yet anyway." Said Mr. Yama. "It seems a change is about to happen. I'm not sure how and I'm not sure why. What we do know is somehow we need you to be here. You were meant to be here," said Mr. Yama, attempting to comfort Akio. "You can stay with Mrs. Fritter and lend me a hand in the mailroom if you like, until we can find out what to do." Mr. Yama looked up at the sky. "It's getting dark, let's get you back to the inn, give you a good supper and then you can get some rest." The two of them stood up and headed back to the inn.

Once they returned, Mrs. Fritter opened the door.

"Come in child," she said to Akio. "You must be hungry. Go and sit down and I'll bring you some stew." Akio went and sat at a big brown table while Mrs. Fritter waddled through a curtain into the kitchen. There were so many different kinds of cutlery on the table, some that Akio had never seen before. A moment later she returned with a big white bowl filled with stew. "Here you are Akio, eat up and then we'll get you up to a room." Akio took hold of one of the spoons and started to dig into the bowl. Tiny hopped off Akio's shoulder and settled himself on the table.

"I should get going," Mr. Yama said to the both of them. "I'll see you tomorrow, Akio. You'll be ok here with Mrs. Fritter." He patted Akio on the shoulder and then left for the night. Mrs. Fritter showed him out and then came back to the table. Akio waffled down the stew and let out a small burp.

"Excuse me," he said.

"Okay my love, let's get you up to a room," said Mrs. Fritter.

"What about the bowl?" asked Akio. Mrs. Fritter then clapped her hands twice slowly. Out from the kitchen came two gloves like Akio had seen in the mailroom. They picked up the bowl and whisked it into the kitchen.

"You have some too?" asked Akio.

"Lots of people do. Well, they did," answered Mrs. Fritter. "Follow me sweetheart."

She led him up the stairs. On the walls were lots of pictures of meadows, beaches and oceans and pictures from cliff tops. They were so beautiful.

"Where did you get these pictures?" asked Akio, looking at each one as he past them.

"I took them and painted them many years ago. Now that I'm a little older, I don't get the time I used to, to do so."

At the top of the stairs, one of the gloves was dusting off some pictures. It dropped the duster on the floor. Akio walked over and handed it back.

"Here you go," he said. The glove took the duster and gave a thumps up, then flew off to dust some more.

"Over here sweetie," Mrs. Fritter called. "This is your room," she said as Akio wandered over. He walked into the room. It had a big wardrobe next to a long chest of drawers. Over in the corner was a nice thick bed with a white sheet and linen. There was a big window over by a door that led to an en-suite bathroom.

"Thank you," Akio said as he sat on the bed.

"I'll see you in the morning my love," said Mrs. Fritter. She then closed the door and went back downstairs. Akio slid off his shoes and lay on the bed. Tiny fluttered up to the end of the bed and curled up. It had been a very strange day. He took off his jumper and saw some pajamas over on a chair. He put them on and climbed into the bed.

"Goodnight Tiny. I suspect if this is just a dream, I will wake up in my own bed in the morning. But then again, perhaps not." he said before lying back and trying to get some sleep.

The next morning, Akio awoke to Tiny lightly chirping at him.

"I guess you're right. Time to get up." He said to Tiny, noticing he was in the same bed. This wasn't a dream then, he was really here.

He got up out of bed and walked into the en-suite. The taps on the sink had clear glass handles with H and C on them. He turned the hot one on and popped the plug in. There was a small washcloth hanging on a rail; he reached over to take it. Tiny then jumped up on the sink and chirped at him before hopping over to a showerhead in the bath.

"You're right. Best to clean properly." He said to Tiny. He then undressed and turned on the shower. It was blindingly cold at first, but didn't take long to get warm.

After his shower Akio went and sat on the bed in his towel.

"Akio my love?" shouted Mrs. Fritter up the stairs. "I've put your clothes in for washing. There's some in the wardrobe you can wear and they should fit ok. They belonged to a boy about your size who stayed here years ago. I put the piece of paper you had in the bedside cabinet." She added. Akio walked over and opened the wardrobe. There were some black trousers hanging next to a nice white shirt. Akio popped them on and noticed a black coat on the door.

"I've left you a pair of black boots just outside your door." shouted Mrs. Fritter again. After putting on the coat, Akio opened the door and picked up the boots. They were big black-laced boots. He put them on and headed downstairs.

Down on the table, Mrs. Fritter had laid out lots of toast and jam.

"Akio," said Mrs. Fritter. "Sit and have some breakfast, and then you best get off to the mailroom, Mr. Yama will be waiting for you." Akio sat down, and Mrs. Fritter placed a plate down for him. He took three pieces of toast and spread on some jam. As he bit into the first piece, his face lit up. It was like nothing he had ever tasted.

"This jam is delicious." He said to Mrs. Fritter, who smiled at him from the kitchen. He quickly finished that piece and moved on to the next two. He pulled a small piece off for Tiny who started to peck away at it. After finishing, Mrs. Fritter handed him some sandwiches wrapped in a paper bag.

"Here's something for your lunch love. I'll see you later."

"Thank you," he said, before leaving the inn for the mailroom.

Along the way, he had a look at all he had rushed past on the trike the day before. There was a bookshop and a florist, a baker, a clothes' shop and a toy maker. Outside the toy maker's, there were two big mechanical bears in red suits, greeting people as they walked in. Walking past, Akio thought to himself that he had to see what was in there, but for now he had to get to the mailroom.

As he approached the mailroom door, a postman ran past him with a huge postbag on his back, knocking Tiny off his shoulder. A letter dropped down from the top of the bag just as the door shut behind him. Akio picked up Tiny, then strolled up and picked up the letter. In dark red, it was addressed to Mrs. Fritter. He slid it into his back pocket and walked into the mailroom.

" Hello, Akio my boy. I take it you met our postman," laughed Mr. Yama.

"Quickly," laughed the postman. "I'd better get going. It was nice to meet you Akio. I'll catch up with you soon." He then picked up his bag, slung it on his back and headed out the door. He didn't stay still for long.

"Now, Akio. Let's get you started. Follow me." Mr. Yama led Akio across the big room to a door that led into the back. What a sight to behold. The door led to a metal balcony, overlooking a huge room with chutes, slides and gloves everywhere.

"Welcome to the world of post," stated Mr. Yama waving his arm over the room.

"Wow," said Akio in awe of such a sight.

"But, we are going over there." Said Mr. Yama, pointing over to the other side of the room. He went over to a ladder leading down, and gestured for Akio to follow him and slid down. Once they reached the bottom they started walking underneath it all over to the other side of the room.

There was a pinewood desk and chair, with a pile of letters next to it.

"Now what I need for you to do for me Akio, is organize all these that have fallen out of the system."

"All these have fallen out? How long have they been here?" asked Akio.

"Some of them for years unfortunately. I never really got the time to sort them; you've seen how fast the post is," answered Mr. Yama. "Okay, I'll leave you to it. I'll be up at the front if you need me."

"Okay Mr. Yama. I think I've got it," said Akio, who then sat down at the desk and started on the pile of letters. Mr. Yama smiled and then headed back to the front of the shop. Tiny hopped off Akio's Shoulder and perched himself on the corner of the desk. This was going to take some time.

A little while later, Akio stopped. He could hear something lightly echoing through the room. He got up, leaving Tiny sleeping on the desk, and went to try and find out what it was and where it was coming from. After following the sound for a while, it was quite clear that it was Mr. Yama's voice, accompanied by another. Akio began to climb up the ladder, but he did it quietly so that no one would hear him. He cracked open the door and peeped through. There was Mr. Yama, and standing in front of the counter was someone in a long black hooded coat with the hood up.

"I must know where he is," said the man in the hood.

"I told you, I don't know where he is. I can't help you." replied Mr. Yama, obviously covering for Akio.

"You'll see that your decision will go against you. He must be found. I heard the boy arrived yesterday. It is imperative that I meet with him. I shall return another time." The man then turned around and walked out of the door.

"Wait! What's happening? Who are you?" shouted Mr. Yama to the man as he left. But it was too late.

Mr. Yama put his head in his hands and let out a big sigh. He looked up and saw Akio at the door.

"Akio. I suppose you heard the end of that," he said. Akio stepped through leaving the door open "I'm going to be honest with you. Please try to understand. It's coming. Whatever it is, it's coming, and I don't know what to do. Someone out there is looking for you, and they know that you are here," Akio gulped and leant on the wall.

"Everything is happening so quickly." Said Akio. "Who am I supposed to be? What am I supposed to do?"

Mr. Yama walked over to the window. He looked up at a mountain towering over the city.

"There is something we can do. But it won't be easy, and I'm not sure I can go with you, or if it will even work," he said.

"What is it? I have to know who I am here," Akio replied. Mr. Yama sat Akio down and started to tell him what he knew.

"The man who prophesized sixteen on sixteen lives up there in the mountain," said Mr. Yama. "You will have to go to him, ask him who you are. I only wish I could give you the answers, Akio. I'm sorry that I can't."

"Why does he live up there?" asked Akio, puzzled.

"He moved up there shortly after he prophesized sixteen on sixteen," said Mr. Yama, coming away from the window. "But I think you going to see him is the only thing we can do." Tiny then flew through the open door and sat next to Akio chirping at him, he could see Akio was upset. He sat and thought for a second. He felt completely lost.

"I wish I'd never taken that bus. I just want to get home." He said to Mr. Yama.

"Akio my boy." Said Mr. Yama placing his hands on Akio's shoulders. "Just remember. What saves a man is to take a step, then another step. It is always the same step, but it gets you to where you are. You took that first step on to that bus, and it led you here, now all you have to do, is keep on stepping, and you'll find yourself to be somewhere else. Life is a journey Akio, and we are the ones who choose where to step next." Akio looked at Mr. Yama, the lost look still covering his face.

"Okay. I'll go and see him," he said.

"You understand Akio, it's not easy up there," said Mr. Yama walking over to the desk. "You'll need some help." Mr. Yama walked over to a drawer. He fumbled around for a bit and then pulled out a white wand. He turned round and presented it to Akio. "This is my old wand. I was practicing wizardry long ago, when I was a young man. A lot of people did, but with the introduction of the glove, people didn't need it anymore, so solo magic was forgotten and the dream weaver invented. Maybe you can use it better than I ever did. Maybe you were supposed to."

17

Akio took the wand from Mr. Yama's hand. The glisten of the white glow reflected off all of the windows when Akio's hand touched it.

"Let's get you ready," said Mr. Yama. "It's time for you to take your next step."

Chapter 2

The Next Step

Mr. Yama closed the mailroom and popped the key in his pocket. Tiny was sat on Akio's shoulder, nestled in Akio's neck, asleep once again.

"Right Akio. Let's head back to the inn and pack you what you'll need," said Mr. Yama to a very quiet Akio. It was a lot for a boy to take in. "We will have to get you a map." He said, trying to think what Akio would need.

"I have one," Akio said to Mr. Yama pulling it out of his pocket. "The bus driver gave me one."

"Oh. That's good then," replied Mr. Yama, who went back to muttering to himself. "You'll need spare shoes, warm clothes, we could find you a warm long coat as well as the one you're wearing," he muttered.

Akio let out a small sigh as they continued to the inn. He had no idea what would be in store for him in the travel to the man of the mountain. There had already been so much information, and he couldn't help but think of home.

"What is this man like?" asked Akio.

"From what I have heard he is a magnificent magician," replied Mr. Yama. "He was apparently the best there was. Although he never agreed with the gloves, said it would make people lazier then magic already did. I suppose in a way, he was right."

"Oh," said Akio quietly. "I assume he will be hard to find?" he asked, hoping to be told otherwise.

"The journey itself will be harder than finding his house; it will be the only one up there. He built it himself." replied Mr. Yama.

Once they arrived back at the inn Mr. Yama went into the kitchen with Mrs. Fritter while Akio waited at the table.

"He came looking for Akio today," Mr. Yama said quietly. "The man in the hood."

Mrs. Fritter gasped and stepped back, leaning on the counter. "We have no other choice, he has to go and see the man in the mountain. He knew this would happen."

Mr. Yama looked through the curtain at Akio and then back at Mrs. Fritter. "He has already agreed to go." Mrs. Fritter placed her hand over her heart.

"Poor boy. Okay. Let's get some things together for him," she said, walking through the curtain. She took Akio's hand and led him into the living room. Then she and Mr. Yama started to fill his pack. Akio wandered upstairs to the bedside cabinet in his room. He knelt down and took out a bag of seed and put it in the front pocket of the coat he was wearing, he remembered he had put it there the other night. He took one last look at the room before closing the door.

Downstairs the two of them were waiting for him, Mr. Yama holding the pack and Mrs. Fritter holding a bag of sandwiches and other such foods. He stepped off the last step, taking the pack from Mr. Yama.

"Here you go dear. Some snacks for the road," said Mrs. Fritter handing him the bag of food.

"It's time, my lad, I know how hard the first step is. But once you take it, all the others seem easier" said Mr. Yama. Akio turned and took a deep breath. At least it was a nice afternoon to start the walk. He put his hand on the doorknob and turned it. He pulled the door open and stepped outside. After stepping outside, he turned his head to Mr. Yama and said.

"You're right. This next step doesn't seem so hard. Thank you guys. I'm sure I'll see you again. At least, I hope to." Akio turned back around and started to walk down the road.

As he reached the pond, Tiny woke up and chirped at him.

"Well, it's about time you woke up," laughed Akio. "You've missed quite a bit, little one. We are on the road to the mountain, to see a very wise man. Hopefully he can tell me what I'm supposed to do about this prophecy business." He sighed.

By dusk Akio had almost reached the edge of the city. He began to feel cold. It was a very different atmosphere here. Houses were more broken down, with not many people living there. So many of the houses and buildings were empty and boarded up and only got worse the closer he got to the bottom of the mountain. Night finally came and Akio decided that they should camp out for the night before taking on the mountain trail.

"Right, Tiny. What we need is some wood, and we can start a nice warm fire," he said taking him off his shoulder. They both started to pick up nearby wood. Tiny's, of course were a lot smaller. Akio piled up the wood into a sort of circle and lit it with the matches from his pack.

"Now that's a lot better isn't it Tiny," he said sitting down. He dipped his hand into his pocket and pulled out the map.

"I don't know how much use this will be my little friend." He opened it up and saw a surprising sight. The paper was bigger, and in addition to the train station he had seen the first time, now it had the train track, the market, Mr. Yama's post, Mrs. Fritter's inn and the pond. It was all there. He couldn't believe it. It seemed he was right about it being no help, due to it only having the places he had already been. He turned and looked at Tiny who had hopped off his shoulder.

"No use looking at this thing I guess," he said. "Bed time." Akio folded up the map and lay down. He put the folded map under his head like a pillow and closed his eyes. Tiny got up and hopped over next to Akio's head and snuggled under his chin and went to sleep. Tomorrow was going to be a big day.

During the night, Akio abruptly awoke. Tiny was next to his head sleeping on his back peacefully. Akio lay back and looked up at the stars. For the first time in the two days he had been in this world, he felt calm and at peace.

He thought about that day he had gotten on that bus, and how if it weren't for Tiny he would be feeling very lonely. But with that little bird by his side, he felt okay.

In the morning, Akio stood at the foot of the mountain looking at two paths, both leading into the mountain.

"I wonder what the difference is between the two paths," he said to Tiny. "I guess we'll just have to take one and see," he added. He looked left, and then looked right. "Well. Right is usually right. Here we go."

Akio set off up the path on the right, entering the forest at the bottom of the mountain. The trees were tall and close together, with the path leading through the middle. There were so many animals that Akio had never seen before, roaming around in the undergrowth and the trees. He sat down on one that had fallen and reached into his pack. He pulled out the sandwiches that Mrs. Fritter had made for him, tore off a piece for Tiny and then dug in himself.

"I hope this trail doesn't go too wide. This mountain is so large it would take ages to walk around it. Although, it's not going to be the easiest of jobs getting close to the top," Akio said to Tiny, who was face deep in his food.

After he had finished, Akio pulled out the long coat from the pack. It looked like it was going to rain. He picked up Tiny and placed him in a front pocket of the coat and slung the pack onto his back. It was going to be a long walk, so each stop could only be for a few minutes.

Later on, Akio had climbed up a tree to try to see where the path was leading. It winded round quite far and then disappeared into the distance. He saw that he was still near to the base of the mountain. It didn't start going up for a while. Akio sighed and headed back down to the ground.

"A while to go yet, Tiny." Tiny let out a disappointing chirp and slumped back into Akio's pocket. It was the afternoon of the second day of traveling, and it seemed they were making no ground.

All too quickly, night came, so Akio decided to stop for the day. He gathered some wood to make another fire.

After it was going, he took the map out once again to make his pillow. Again the map had added the places he had been. Although it did show another split in the road.

"I don't believe it." He said to Tiny. "We have to choose a way again." Frustrated, Akio folded the map back up and lay down with it under his head. He wrapped himself up in the coat with Tiny still in the pocket. He closed his eyes and drifted off to sleep.

At the break of dawn, Tiny was already awake, frantically chirping at Akio and jumping on his chest. Akio rubbed his eyes and sat up.

"What's wrong Tiny?" But as he turned his head, he saw the reason why. Crouched over by a hazel bush, was a poised tiger, waiting patiently. Slowly Akio moved placing his feet up right, he was still crouched down as not to seem threatening. He held Tiny tight in his hands. Then without a second thought, Akio turned and ran. Quickly the tiger followed. Akio's heart was beating as fast as his legs were running, with Tiny hiding away in Akio's palm. As he ran, faster and faster, Akio was muttering to himself.

"Don't look back. Just don't look back." But his head couldn't seem to help the curiosity. He turned his head to see the tiger roaring behind him. As he turned his head back quickly, an unseen branch knocked him to the floor. With Tiny still strongly clutched in his hands he rolled on to his front and moved to his knees. Sure enough there was the tiger, waiting, just in front of him. The moment was tense. What to do now? Akio thought. Then, the tiger leapt into the air, straight for Akio, but before they could hit, the same black hooded figure that had been in Mr. Yama's post appeared as if from nowhere, and collided with the tiger. They both hit the ground and Akio ran for cover. Behind a tree, Akio and Tiny looked on. Both the hooded man and the tiger stood and circled each other. The tiger ran for the man, who in that split second threw out his arm, and out of his hand came a red-misted dust. The tiger instantly fell to the ground. Akio looked at the figure he had previously been told to fear. He stood tall, in a long leather coat, very similar to Akio's. The black hood covering his head came for underneath the coat and had a red lining on the inside. He wore a balaclava covering his face and held a tall, black and red shining staff.

"Come out from behind that tree Akio, I can assure you the tiger is well-sedated," said the hooded man, turning towards Akio. "I expect that's the first time something like that has ever happened to you. Well, you will have to get used to that sort of thing here in this world. And I'm telling you now, it gets worse, I promise you that."

Akio stepped out and walked closer.

"Who are you? And should my heart be filled with fear or thanks?" Akio said curiously. The man let out a short laugh and took a step closer to Akio. He leant over.

"I'm not here to hurt you Akio. I'm here to help you reach the man of the mountain. If I wasn't here to help you--" the man turned away, "--You'd be dead." Akio took a big gulp, realizing the magnitude of what had just happened. The hooded man turned back and took a look around.

"The creatures of this world move quickly. As should we, come on." He then beckoned Akio to start walking behind him. There was still a while to go and Akio didn't really want to continue traveling alone. So he did.

As he followed behind the hooded man, he tried to get a look at his face. But each time the man noticed him doing so, turned his head as not to be seen. This man was very mysterious, and hadn't said a word since they had set off together.

"So, you live here then," said Akio, trying to start up somewhat of a conversation.

"For the last ten years, yes," he replied without even a turn of the head. "I was new to this world then too, as you are now."

"This is Tiny," said Akio turning towards the little bird, which was perched on his shoulder. The man stopped and turned around holding out his finger.

"Hello Tiny," he said stroking Tiny's chin. Akio was surprised. Something changed in the man's eyes in that moment. They turned soft and Akio sensed a hint of loss in the man's heart.

"You don't have many friends, do you?" asked Akio. The man took his hand away, still looking at Tiny.

"No, no I don't. I lost a very dear friend a long time ago. And I can see you two have a similar bond. Hold on to your friends, Akio." The man then strolled on through the trees. Akio looked at Tiny and realized that what had previously been thought of the hooded figure was a big misconception of the truth, and that which he had just learned would only be the tip of the iceberg.

The man seemed somewhat distant after the encounter with Tiny. It seemed that Akio was not the only one who felt a sense of loneliness in this world.

It was the late afternoon, when the hooded man stopped at an entrance to a cave. Akio stopped behind him and looked into the eerie path.

"We're going, in there?" gulped Akio.

"If you want to get to your destination as quickly as possible, yes." Akio looked once again at the cave.

"Do you know what's in there? Is it safe?" The hooded man turned to Akio and sighed.

"No, I don't. Look Akio, you're going to have to learn. In this world, you sometimes have to take a chance to get the outcome you're looking for, or to where you want to be. It's about taking that next step." Akio remembered what Mr. Yama had said about taking the next step. "Now are you ready?" The hooded man asked.

"Yes, I suppose I am," replied Akio. The hooded man then tapped his staff on the floor, which made the tip light up.

"Let's go then," he said.

"I'm going to have to know what to call you," said Akio as they walked into the cave. The man looked slightly round and said, "Yes I suppose you will. These days I go by the name Raven."

"These days?" Asked Akio. "So you were someone else before?"

"I do not give my name anymore. For reasons you won't understand. Not yet anyway," the man replied. Akio thought to himself for a moment before catching up closer to Raven and asked, "Do you know about this prophecy?"

The man laughed and said, "Oh yes, I know all about it."

"Then you can tell me about it," Akio said excitedly. But Raven stayed quiet before saying,

"I'm not sure I should be the one to tell you. Even if I was, this isn't the place." Raven kept on saying that. What was it Akio was not ready to know yet?

A little while later they walked through an arch into a big echoic part of the cave, with a path that led down around the outside.

"Let's get to the bottom and stop for the evening. This cut through has helped and we are now making good time." said Raven, who continued on down the path.

"And then will you tell me?" asked Akio.

"Maybe," murmured Raven. They then made their way to the bottom.

Once there, Raven found a big area and told Akio to find some wood.

"You stay here Tiny," said Akio putting Tiny down on a nearby stone. Akio then walked off trying to find some wood. It was understandably hard to find in this sort of environment. But after a while of looking he saw a few wooden crates piled on each other. He picked up two and started to kick the other one back to Raven.

"I found these," he said to Raven once he returned. "I think there may be things inside," he added. Raven took up his staff and smashed two of them open, breaking them into pieces.

"Old pots. I suspect they've been here a while," said Raven gathering the wood. Tiny hopped onto the third and started pecking it with his beak.

"We'll do that one later Tiny. Come over here," said Akio. Raven piled up the wood and then held out his hand. A small flame appeared in his palm, which then got bigger. As it reached full size he threw it onto the wood making the fire.

"Come and take a seat, Akio," said Raven sitting down. Akio and Tiny went over and sat opposite Raven, who had pulled an envelope from this coat. He took his staff and tapped it on the opening. A misty picture of a loaf of bread came out of the envelope, which Raven then moved into the fire. He then stabbed the bottom end of his staff into the fire, pulling out a real loaf of bread.

"So your staff is like a dream weaver," said Akio, as he had seen that kind of magic before.

"Not quite," said Raven. "Although similar, it's a lot more powerful. Now, you asked about the prophecy." Raven handed Akio the bread and broke off a piece for Tiny. "Akio, I can't tell you much, but what I can tell you is a war is coming. You will have to learn how to use the wand you were given. Use magic spells and learn how to fight. You must learn how to use advanced magic, and most of all, how to take a life."

"How did you know I have a wand?" asked Akio. The man reached into Akio's coat and pulled the wand out.

"You'll find I know a lot about you, Akio. But that isn't important now. You get some sleep, and I'll stay on watch," said Raven, who then made a fireball and started to float it around in the air. Tiny hopped onto Akio and snuggled for the night. Raven looked on with a smile on his face.

Back at the inn Mrs. Fritter and Mr. Yama were sitting by the fire, drinking cocoa.

"I do hope he's okay," said Mrs. Fritter clutching her mug.

"I'm sure he'll be fine. He has a strong heart," replied Mr. Yama touching his hand to her shoulder. "He has taken to all this surprisingly well."

"Still, he's only a boy." Mrs. Fritter stood up. "I think I'll make another pot of cocoa. I need to take my mind off of this." She left the room and headed for the kitchen. Just then, there was a knock on the door. Mr. Yama went to answer it. When he opened the door, there was a glove holding a letter. Mr. Yama took the letter and then closed the door.

"A letter. It's addressed to both of us," shouted Mr. Yama to the kitchen. He went back, sat down and opened it.

"Read it out." Mrs. Fritter shouted back." Mr. Yama took out the paper and started to read.

"Do not be alarmed. I have located Akio, and he has come to no harm. I will lead him to the man of the mountain, and will protect him with my life. Things are about to change, and suggest you prepare for the events to come. Raven." Mr. Yama sat back. "Do we know a Raven?" asked Mr. Yama.

"Not that I know of. He sounds nice though. At least he will be protected from all the things out there, that hooded figure for one," replied Mrs. Fritter. Mr. Yama looked out of the window and thought to himself. He knew Akio's heart was strong, but couldn't help agree with Mrs. Fritter. He hoped he was okay.

The next day in the mountain, Akio was woken by a kick from Raven.

"It's time to move," he said, pulling his staff out of the ground. Akio poked a sleeping Tiny.

"Time to go, Tiny," said Akio picking him up.

"Stay close," said Raven. "There is something else in here, and I don't think it's far away. If I tell you to get down, you listen." Akio popped Tiny in his coat and walked very closely behind Raven. Raven was constantly looking around. Akio sensed that he was worried. There were statues down a long corridor they had walked into. Akio looked at each one as he past it. They were statues of past warriors, noblemen of old. They then came to a big lake and Raven stopped suddenly when he heard a rock fall.

"Stop, Akio. Find cover, now." Akio ran over behind a bolder near the lake. Raven turned his head and looked back. Out from where they had come, the statues had come to life. They ran at Raven swinging their swords. Raven threw off his coat and raised his staff into the air. One by one Raven smashed the statues away, but numbers started to take advantage. Raven threw spell after spell, but all were too small to crumble the enemy.

"Akio! Into the lake, go under and to the other side. Get out of here!" shouted Raven. Akio stood and leaped into the lake. He held Tiny tight above the water. When he got to the other side, he turned to see Raven. The statues were knocking him around.

"Raven!" he shouted.

"Get out of here Akio!" Raven shouted back. Akio turned and ran out of the cave. When he got out, there was snow under foot. He put Tiny down on a nearby branch.

"Stay here," he said, before running back into the cave. As he made it back to the lake, Raven let out an almighty shout. A great big ball of red light exploded out from Raven's body, throwing the statues against the walls, smashing them to pieces. Raven then rose up and flew directly at the wall to the exit, smashing his way through. Akio ran back outside and saw Raven collapsed on the ground. He ran over to see if he was still breathing. Thankfully he was and Akio pulled Raven up onto his knees.

"Why didn't you do that sooner?" asked Akio.

"Using too much magic will signify your position. They cannot find you, Akio. Or they will kill you," Raven responded weakly. He pulled himself to his feet and straightened his garments.

"Right. Let's keep going," he said, picking his staff up off the floor. Akio was dumbfounded. Raven seemed fine. Confused a little more, Akio took Tiny and put him back on his shoulder before following after Raven again.

"We are almost there, Akio. But that doesn't mean you are any safer. We must get you inside his house first." Akio and Raven set off again, now in a new, snowy atmosphere. There was snow on the ground as far as the eye could see, but the sun was out and was as warm as a summer's day. And even though it hadn't and wasn't raining, there was rainbow overhead. The more Akio saw of this world, the more beautiful it was. Only made darker by the creatures that roamed. As beautiful as this world was, it could not take away from the reason Akio was here. As they got over the hill, in the distance Akio saw a small wood cabin. Finally they had nearly reached the destination. But the joy would only last for a short while. As a pack of wolves, each one the size of a bear, appeared surrounding them. Tiny started to shake, as Akio stood there frozen.

"Mountain wolves. Take out your wand Akio and say the words 'Elissia protecto'." Akio took out his wand and said the words he had been told. An energy beam surrounded his body and Raven crouched a little. He hit the ground with his staff and shouted, "Bakhan!"

The snow, wolves and Akio were flung into the air, Raven flew up and grabbed Akio and flew him over to the cabin. They lightly floated down to the ground and landed at the door. A huge sense of relief came over Akio. He was finally there and could find out who he was. Raven took the protective ray off of Akio and went and knocked on the door.

"It's me," he said. The door was then opened as if by magic.

"Go in," said Raven to Akio. Akio took a breath and walked in the door. Again, the inside was a lot bigger than what the outside had shown. Raven came in closing the door behind him. As he did, a protective ray covered the house.

Over by a desk in the corner sat an elderly gentleman. The elderly man turned in his chair. He looked down his glasses and said, "Hello Akio, I've been waiting for you.

This is a very big day." Akio walked over and took Tiny in his hands.

"Forgive my insisting sir, but can you tell me who I am, who Raven is and why I'm here?" he said. The man got up off his chair and walked over to three chairs near a table.

"Of course my boy, come sit down, and I'll tell you all about it." Akio went over and put Tiny down on the table. Raven stayed over in the corner, slumped in his own chair.

"Now," said the man. "My name is Teju. Long ago I learned of what was to come. But when I told people of the events yet to happen, they laughed me out of the city. But then, sure enough, a boy came to me and told me that he was not of this world. It was then I knew what would happen. I took him in and sheltered him from the world. Not long after, a war started for the rule of the realm. But with the boy hidden, nothing could happen, so seemed to die down. Ten years have passed, and the war still lingers. When I heard of your arrival, I knew I had to get you here." Akio started to fill in the gaps. "Stand up and tell the boy who you are," he said to Raven.

Raven stood up and took off the coat. He then lowered his hood to reveal long, rusty-coloured blonde hair and striking eyes. Akio gasped in amazement.

"My name." Said Raven. "Is Akio. I have been in this world for ten years. I failed in my years to end the wars, for with me in hiding, they never happened. But you must succeed where I did not. I am you, and you are I. We are one. The one." Akio sat back in his chair with his jaw dropped in disbelief. As much as he didn't want to believe it, he couldn't help but notice the identical features to his own. The man stood in front of him was most certainly himself.

"The war is coming very soon Akio. Soon enough it will take over," said Teju. "We must find out what has gone wrong all these years, and put an end to these wars. It seems a circle has occurred, a glitch in time that has brought you here. It means the war must happen, and you must finish it." Tiny looked at Akio, and then at the man who called himself Raven. He then proceeded to faint on the table. Akio took him in his hands and held him tight. This was most certainly a lot to take in.

Chapter 3

Past And Present

Akio got up out of his chair.

"Wait. You have to explain this in more detail," he said with an ultimately horrified look on his face.

"Okay okay, sit down Akio. You have to calm down," said Teju. "I know it's a lot to take in." Akio sat back down with Tiny still in his hands.

"Skye City is only the beginning. There is so much more beyond this mountain. Now, listen carefully for there is still a lot for you to hear. The spirit Michael years ago was the founder of this entire place. He crafted it in his perfect image piece by piece. But, unfortunately there was another. Raphael was Michael's brother, and Michael had entrusted him to help shape the perfect world. But the power was too much for Raphael to handle. He wanted more, he wanted rule over his own world. They fought over this for some time until, unknowingly to Michael, Raphael delved into darker magic and the underworld was created, a dark and cold place where people could seek power and lust in their own greed. As hard as it was, Michael had no choice but to banish Raphael to this dark and barren place, to rot in his own creation. Unwisely, Michael assumed that would be the last of it. But Raphael had sworn his revenge. He kept to his promise. Over the years, darkness grew and spread across the land. He has gained followers, those he granted power in order to destroy the light. You, Akio are what binds good and evil, and it is down to you to make a choice. I was foolish to try and shelter you the first time. You are the missing piece of the puzzle. I believe both of you are able to end this war." Akio was speechless.

"So they know I'm here?" asked Akio worriedly.

"I'm afraid they do. It is why since you got here, things have tried to kill you. Raphael knows he cannot let you live again. Now that there are two of you, the threat towards him is twice as large" Raven walked over to Akio and knelt in front of him.

"I will teach you all I know. Then we will take this on together. You are not alone in this." Akio picked Tiny up off of the table and stroked the back of his head.

"Can't Michael do something about it?" asked Akio.

"No one has seen Michael since Raphael's return," said Teju looking out a window. "If he were here I'm sure he would have intervened." He shook his head to snap out of it and continued. "You and Tiny are welcome to stay here while you learn the ways of the world. I have already prepared a room for you, you should find it very much to your liking."

"Thank you sir," said Akio still stroking Tiny's head. "If you two don't mind, I think Tiny and I will retire to our room. I have to put things into place. If I could use some paper to send a letter, I'm sure Mr. Yama and Mrs. Fritter will be wondering how I am." Teju and Raven looked at each other.

"I think for now they are best left in the dark about what's happening. When the time is right, I will contact them myself as not to worry them," said Teju standing up to lead Akio to his room. "Follow me Akio. I'll take you to your room so you can get some good rest for tomorrow."

Teju lead Akio up a long staircase and down a wide corridor. He stopped and opened a big wooden door. The room was very big, with a big bed against the back wall. In the corner of the room, sat a big long bookcase filled with books. The books were mostly magic books. There was a big rug on the floor, a wardrobe filled with clothes and a little bed on a bedside table for Tiny. Tiny chirped happily out of Akio's hands and into his bed. Akio could see that Tiny felt right at home.

"I'll make sure that Tiny is looked after during days you are learning with Raven." said Teju still standing in the doorway. "I'll see you in the morning." Teju left and closed the door. Akio sat on the bed and slipped off his shoes. He lay down and closed his eyes. Things were going to change from here on out.

Close to a year past and Raven would spend hours a day teaching Akio about the world and how to use his magic and raise his power. They battle trained and practiced magic spells. Akio would sit and read through books filled with magic and books about different creatures he would see in this world. Tiny spent his time with Teju helping with daily chores. He would often sit with Akio while he read. Teju would write to Mr. Yama and Mrs. Fritter every now and again, telling of Akio's well-being, but mentioned nothing of Raven or the teachings Akio was receiving. He would tell them each time the war drew closer, and implored them to prepare and warn others. Akio took to the lessons well, just as Raven had before. The more time went on Teju would reveal more to Mrs. Fritter and Mr. Yama. He would also sometimes write other letters and send them north. Akio wondered where those ones were going. As the end of the year drew near, Akio had come a long way. Raven presented Akio with his own black, hooded coat and a holster to carry his wand. Over the past year, times had become darker and the time to start planning the next part of the journey was getting near. The end of the year came and as the sun set Raven called the finish of another day.

"You have done very well and come a long way. Your power has risen exceptionably," said Raven as the two of them sat on the edge of the hill.

"Really?" asked Akio, pleased with himself.

"Well. As you know, every being that ever lived runs on energy; it's what gives us the power to walk, run, fight and all other manner of things. During growth it increases. With a strong heart and solid mind, that power can be increased even further, some a lot more than others. You will learn to use it and control it. Soon you will be able to sense another's power, you will feel it. That is how I found you when you first arrived here. But in some, power can and has been given. Men in search of power gave themselves to Raphael; he bred and merged them with the dead and created a powerful race of undead rogues." Akio listened intently.

"How powerful are they? And how powerful are you?" he asked.

"Compared to some of them I'm still near the bottom rung," replied Raven. "It's not something commonly spoken about. But you, Akio, you will find the power I never found."

"I would ask you what is to come. But I guess they are set to change," said Akio, holstering his wand.

"The war is close, Akio, and we must do our best to keep it away from putting an end to this world. But yes, they would have begun to change the day you arrived." Raven stood up once again and asked Akio to do the same.

"Now, for a final spell. All great warriors need a trusty steed to lead them into battle. Retrieve Tiny please," said Raven, looking over at the cabin. Akio jogged inside and brought Tiny outside. Raven took Tiny and put him on his finger.

"Tiny, would you like to help Akio?" he asked. Tiny chirped happily in an agreeing tone. "Okay then, let's do this." Raven put Tiny down and turned to Akio. "Okay Akio. I want you to point your wand at Tiny and say the word 'formination'." Akio took out his wand and pointed it at Tiny. He said the word and the end of his wand lit up. Tiny began to grow and change. In a flash, there stood Tiny, a big and powerful bird with a beautiful head, wing and tail feathers.

"Behold your noble steed," said Raven. "To change him back, just say the same." Raven handed Akio a small silver whistle. "To call to him, blow this whistle. And I'm sure he will oblige. If he's not with you already." Akio stood in wonder of what Tiny had become. He went up and stroked his neck.

"Wow, look at you Tiny," he said, brushing his hands through Tiny's feathers. Tiny leant down and stroked his face to Akio's. He then pushed Akio onto his back at took to the sky. They soared higher and higher, faster and faster. Akio threw his arms back and felt the wind flow through his hair and on his face. Tiny flew up and then began to circle back to the ground. They landed down by Raven and Akio jumped off.

"Come on Akio, let's get a bite to eat. We need to set off in the morning," said Raven heading to the cabin. Akio put Tiny back to normal and they both then headed inside. Teju had prepared dinner, which was waiting on the table. Tiny immediately dove head-first into a bowl of seeds. They all sat down at the table and started to dig in.

"Okay boys. Remember when you're out there, things will be after you." He turned to Akio. "Only use Tiny when you have to, you don't want to draw to much attention. Not in the beginning of your journey." Teju sat back and addressed them both. "You must head to the city of Danathor to inform the king. The black castle of the underworld is breeding an army. Dark creatures guard the realm day and night. They are the dark knights of the underworld. Made from the envy in Raphael's heart. Creatures that have sought out power. We also have to remember that a year has passed and the enemy is moving ever closer. Rogues are swarming from the depths of the underworld." Raven looked at Akio and then at Teju.

"We are ready Teju," he said sitting up in his seat. Teju smiled before finishing his dinner. Tiny popped his head out of the empty bowl and let out a small burp. Akio swallowed his last bit of food before sitting back in his chair. The sun had set on another day and the time had come to finally move.

During the night Akio didn't sleep very well. He woke up in a sweat and sat up. He had been having a recurring dream of what was to come. He looked over at Tiny who was sleeping peacefully. He heard a noise and looked round. It sounded like it had come from outside. Akio got out of bed and slowly moved over to the window. He looked through and saw Raven standing outside in the rain. He was just standing there on the edge of the hill. Akio stood and watched a little longer, but Raven didn't move a muscle. He then looked round and saw Akio standing at his window. A red aura then burst around Raven's body before he flew off into the distance. He was indeed very powerful. Akio had a lot to live up to. Raven had become a powerful man in the eleven years he had been here, but Akio couldn't help but wonder what it was that had changed him, and would change Akio into the man he had been taught by the past year. It was a worrying thought.

Morning dawned and Raven had not been back all night. But then from downstairs.

"Akio!" He shouted up the stairs. "Suit up. Its time to go!" Akio got out of bed and opened the wardrobe. He pulled out some black trousers and a black long sleeved shirt. He slipped on the trousers and the two long black pull on boots and put a layer of armor on under the shirt. He put a silver glove gauntlet on each hand and put on the silver boot guards. He attached his wand to his belt and put on his hooded coat, it too like Raven's had a red lining inside the hood. He pulled the hood over his head and looked at himself in the mirror. He looked like Raven had the first day they had met. It was all happening. Akio went downstairs to find Raven and Tiny already waiting for him.

"Remember. Only use stronger magic if you have to. Raphael's sense is strong and he will be able to sense when excessive magic is used. He's trying to find you," said Teju. "Now there is certainly no time to lose. You'd best be on your way. Take this." Teju handed Raven a letter. "Give this to the king when you arrive." Raven slipped the letter inside his cloak and took hold of his staff; he gestured for Akio to head outside. Akio held out his finger for Tiny who hopped on up to his shoulder. He then opened the door and stepped out. At that moment, a huge ball and chain struck the ground right in front of him. Akio leapt to the side just in time for it to miss. Tiny was thrown from his shoulder and was caught by Raven standing in the doorway. Akio looked up from the floor and over the hill walked a shadowed creature, wearing black amour and who had a grotesque face with scratches and scuffs all over its body.

"Akio! Watch out!" shouted Raven. The creature swung the long ball and chain again which crashed down next to him. Akio rolled out of the way and onto his feet. Raven went to run and help, but Akio, now standing, took up his wand. The look in his eyes had changed. He destroyed the ball chain with a rush of magic. Raven stopped and looked on as Akio, strolling strongly towards the beast, shot another blue beam spell, which knocked the creature into the air. He came crashing down and Akio shot another, throwing the monster backwards into a tree, knocking it from its roots. As the beast stood up again Akio pointed his wand.

He shouted, letting out an almighty surge of energy, which crashed into the creature, turning him to dust. When all settled, Akio dropped to his knees, looking at his hands and his wand with his now more-normal eyes. It was like Raven had said a year ago, about learning to take a life. Raven ran over placing his hand on Akio's shoulder.

"By the gods. How did you summon such power?" asked Raven in shock.

"I don't know. It seems a blur. I didn't mean for that to..." muttered Akio. Raven knelt beside him.

"It may be in your heart to show mercy. But you will receive none and cannot afford to give any Akio. You must trust your judgment. It will flow through you strongly. You won't accept it straight away. But like I said, at some point you had to learn to take a life. Now, we must make haste." Raven helped Akio to his feet. He holstered his wand and stood up. "This is only a taste of what is to come," added Raven.

The two then said their goodbyes to Teju and set of for the kingdom of Danathor.

Meanwhile, deep in the land of darkness and destruction, an almighty scream of anger came from the black castle.

"He was destroyed?" shouted the voice. "He's only been here a year. How could he have the strength already to defeat a rogue?"

"My lord Raphael, we have sent hordes of rouges to the east and west." said Vigo, servant to Raphael. Raphael turned and sat on his throne.

"It seems time has already been altered. The boy is much stronger than his past self. It seems it will be even harder this time around to kill him." Raphael pondered. "We do have the advantage. We have past experience, we have lived through this before, and we know where we can hurt him." Raphael stood up. "This time. We shall succeed."

Back on the mountain trail, Akio, Tiny and Raven had reached the Jota River.

"Looks like we are going to need a boat," said Raven, looking around.

"Why can't we just walk with the river?" Akio asked.

"Water moves swiftly, and if we walked the entire way, you wouldn't have the strength to combat what we would find at the end, or even on the way," replied Raven, pulling a fallen tree trunk over to the water.

"Oh," said Akio. Raven took out his staff and waved it over the trunk. The wood began to move and shape-shift, creating a boat.

"Hop in, kid," said Raven, jumping into the boat.

Once Akio and Tiny had got in, Raven leant backwards and put the tip of his staff in the water. It bubbled up and gave the boat a push forward, and off they went down the river. As the boat traveled down the river, Akio sat back. He wondered what else this world had to offer; it still, after the past year, had a surprise round every corner. Tiny hopped off Akio's shoulder and perched himself on the side of the boat.

"Can I ask you something, Raven?" asked Akio, sitting up.

"You may," replied Raven, still laid back in the boat. Akio paused for a moment, and then asked.

"What was it that happened, that got us stuck here?" Raven sat up.

"It's not an easy story to tell, as I don't really know. Maybe the loss and betrayal we saw. I got something wrong. I missed something, and I've been here ever since." A sad look overtook Raven's face, and he lay back down. "It's not important now Akio. It is now set to change anyway. Get what rest you can, the boat will take us where we need to be."

Akio leant back. Maybe it was too early to ask that question. After all, he was sure at some point he would find out.

Night came swiftly and Akio and Raven floated along down the Jota River. It was quiet. All that could be heard was the water rippling past. Raven sharply sat up.

"What is it?" asked Akio staying low in the boat. They looked over to the shore and saw a hoard of Cyclopes running through the wood. They were heading west.

"The creatures have begun to move. Raphael has made the call." Raven looked over at Akio. "The War is starting. Creatures will start to choose their side. It seems the Cyclopes are moving." He looked back at the shore. "But which side have they chosen? Get some sleep Akio. At this pace we should be reaching the Green Valley by morning." Akio rolled over and closed his eyes, while Raven stayed awake, keeping watch over the boat.

By morning, just as Raven had said, the boat had reached the valley.

"Wake up Akio, it's time to start walking again." Akio sat up and was met by the beautiful sight that was the Green Valley. Raven had just finished writing a letter, which he put in an envelope. He turned to Tiny who had just woken up. "Tiny? I need you to do an important job for me." Tiny hopped up in excitement. "Do you remember your way back from the tip of the river?" Tiny chirped happily. "I need you to take this letter to Teju, it's very important." Tiny took the letter in his beak and flapped over to Akio. He rubbed against his cheek to say goodbye and then flew off up the river. "Don't worry Akio, He'll be okay. Now we have to move on, if we walk all day we should reach Danathor by the early evening." Raven took out his staff and put the boat back to normal as a tree trunk, and then they both started their walk through the valley.

"So, Danathor? Is that the kingdom for this world?" asked Akio. "I still don't know a lot about here."

"One of them," replied Raven, playing with another ball of fire.

"One of them?" Akio asked.

"Danathor is the kingdom that governs the land to the south. Skye City, the mountains and where we are right now, are all under the power of Danathor," explained Raven. "Beyond that is miles of fields and forest land. Then to the east and west lie cities, kingdoms and other such surprises. Far past the land of Hera in the north lies the darkened sky. That is where the black gates of the underworld hold evils crueler than you can imagine. After we have informed all we can, that is our destination." Raven then started to walk a little ahead. There was still a long journey ahead of them.

Along the walk, Akio was practicing his magic. Just as Raven did, he summoned a small ball of fire and started waving it back and forth.

"I can't get it as big Raven," he said letting it fade away. Raven continued on but lifted his head to say,

"Concentrate, Akio. Feel the power within. Trust that feeling." Akio stopped and closed his eyes. He cupped his hands together and concentrated. The wind picked up and swooshed through the trees. Raven stopped up ahead and turned around. A red glow had outlined Akio and the sky began to dim. A small fireball materialized in his hands as the red glow grew. The fireball grew and grew as Raven stood in awe of what he was seeing. Then with an explosion of power Raven was thrown backwards and the fireball engulfed the surrounding trees.

"Akio! Stop!" He shouted. "It's getting too powerful." But Akio could not hear him. Raven stood up and tried to get in closer, but as Akio rose up into the air the red aura prevented him from getting any closer. Trees were ablaze and the fire was growing still. Then in blink of an eye, it stopped and Akio fell to the floor. Raven whipped out his staff and put out the surroundings before running over to a limp Akio.

"Akio? Can you hear me? Akio?" He turned him over. He wasn't breathing. Raven raised his arm in the air and sharply hit Akio's chest. He instantly sat up and coughed to catch his breath.

"What, by the gods, was that?" Raven asked, still amazed at what had transpired.

"I just did what you told me to," said Akio. "I focused my energies and concentrated on the power inside. But it started to take over and was too much to control." Raven helped him to his feet and brushed him off.

"Well, as much as I'd like to let you rest, time won't wait for us. We have to move on." Raven was still amazed at how powerful Akio seemed. There was something different about the younger version of himself. Something darker, maybe.

Back at Teju's cottage, Tiny had flown throughout the day and night and was exhausted when he arrived. He landed on the windowsill and tapped the window with his beak. Teju came to the window and saw Tiny leaning against the frame.

"Tiny," he said opening the window. "Come in come in. You look tired." Tiny hopped in and over to the table. He held up his head and chirped with the letter still clutched in his beak.

"What's this, then," he said, taking it from Tiny. He opened it up and began to read. As he got further through, the look on his face turned to that of concern. "So. The creatures are on the move. It's just like last time." Tiny hopped closer to Teju trying to glance at the letter but Teju moved over to the window. "The war is finally starting. Even after eleven years, I still am not ready."

Teju started to pack a bag. It was time to go back to Skye City. It had been a long time.

That night Raven and Akio had reached the hillside looking over the kingdom of Danathor, a little later than Raven had predicted and he hoped that people would still be awake. Akio looked down the hillside. Danathor lay across a river with walls spanning the vast city. It looked older than Skye City, mostly made of stone with the castle in the centre. They proceeded down the hill and to the big walls of stone. Raven took up his staff and banged on the thick wooded doors. A guard appeared in the lookout.

"Raven, you're back," said the guard happily. "Open the gates!" he shouted to the guards at the gate. Raven and Akio stepped back as the big wooden gates started to open.

"It's great to see you again Raven and with company, I see," said the guard.

"I'm afraid not, Norx. The news I bring is not good. Is the king still available?" he said shaking hands.

"He is," replied Norx. "Follow me."

He led them through the courtyard and through the old town market. They went over the bridge and down a long corridor over to a spiral stone staircase. It went up for ages it seemed, but on noticing through a window, Akio saw it led to the castle. They came to the main chamber doors. It was so different to everything else Akio had seen. On entering, Akio stood in awe. Over at the end of the room sitting on a high throne was a man with long grey hair and a dark beard in a dark green robe. He raised his head and on noticing Raven, stood and made his way across the room.

"Raven. You have returned. Is it time?" he said worriedly, clutching at Raven's hand.

"I'm afraid so, Garron. But how did you know?" Garron smiled and pulled out a letter.

"From Teju. He has already informed me." Raven turned to Akio.

"This is Akio." Garron walked over to Akio and placed his hands on his shoulders.

"My boy. I have heard your story, time and time over. Waiting for the day I could finally meet you. But may I ask. Why is it that you are eleven year's late?" Raven looked at Akio and shook his head insistently.

"I'm afraid I don't know, sir. A lot is still new to me." What had he meant by late?

"Garron. My friend. We have traveled long to get here and are in need of rest, and in my haste to get here, I foolishly forgot food. We have lived off the scraps we could find as didn't want to use too much magic. May we rest and then eat with you in the morning. I feel it can wait till then," said Raven trying to drive the conversation away.

"Why did you not want to use a lot of magic?" asked Garron.

"I'm afraid I was not able to, I'll explain later," Raven replied.

"Certainly, I'll have beds made for you both and in the morning we shall feed you well." Akio was glad, it had been tiring and after what had happened in the forest, he hadn't had a proper night's sleep. They were led to their chamber where they lay their heads and got some sleep.

Morning came and the sun shone in Teju's cottage windows. He went over and woke up Tiny, who was sleeping on a pillow.

"Time to go, little one. I'll need to ride you if you don't mind. It will be a lot quicker that way. They will not be tracking us. It is only Akio that worries them. For now at least." The two headed outside with the bag Teju had packed the previous night. He waved his wand and Tiny transformed. He jumped on his back.

"Fly fast, Tiny. Time is precious to us now."

Chapter 4

United Either Side

Tiny flew as fast as he could back to Skye City. The enemy had started moving and it was time to unite for the good. It had been a long time since Teju had been back, and he feared that people would still distrust him. He knew of at least two people he could go to first, as they had met the boy when he first arrived. He couldn't help wonder what would happen this time around. He had sheltered Akio from harm the first time, and things had already changed. He looked down to the ground, and sure enough creatures were moving. Luckily it was not in the direction of Skye City. Soon enough, they would be heading back in larger numbers and would be on the attack. It started to rain so Teju leant in closer to Tiny and pulled up his hood. There was still a way to go.

Meanwhile in Danathor, Akio sat up in his bed. He looked over to the windowsill and saw that Raven was still asleep. He decided to get up anyway and have a look around. He put on his clothes and headed out the door. He made his way through the castle and peered upon a circular room. He went back, and walked in. In the middle of the room stood a stone plinth holding a magnificent sword holstered in a shield.

"Beautiful, isn't it," said a voice. Akio turned to see a young woman in a long sky-blue dress standing in the doorway.

"It certainly is," replied Akio as she came and stood beside him. Akio looked around. "What are these writings on the walls?" he asked looking back at the young woman.

"It is the story behind our kingdom, our people and this world." The woman walked over to the wall and brushed her hand over the words.

"What does it say?" Akio asked, intrigued. The woman walked back over to Akio and turned to the sword and shield.

"It tells of the betrayal to Michael from Raphael, the splitting of the world, the start of the darkness and the battle they fought against each other. It moves onto the attempts for Raphael to gain more power." She walked over to the plinth and up to the shining weapons. "Left weak, Michael disappeared, but not before presenting Danathor with a gift. His sword and his shield. But alas, his plan did not work," she continued, dropping her head. "It is said that only one can wield the two. But no such person has come." She stopped and looked at Akio. Akio stood still as she whisked her way back over to him. "A man in a black cloak. Would you be Akio?" His eyes widened and he stumbled back. How did she know his name?

"I am," he said with a shaky voice.

"Then you have the power to control them. Go on touch them. Awaken them from their rest," she insisted. Hesitant, Akio moved forward. He held his hand out as he stepped up to the plinth. The sword and shield started to glow as he neared. Closer and closer he got and the more and more the glow beamed out in the room. But when he had gotten too close he was thrown backwards by a rush of energy.

"I don't understand." said the woman, running to Akio's aid. "You are Akio aren't you? And you're wearing a black cloak. It's supposed to all fit."

"He is." Said Raven leant at the door. "But he is not ready yet. The sword and shield know this." The woman looked up.

"It's been a long time, Raven."

"It has, Yolanda. I think we should feed our young hero don't you think?" Raven pulled Akio to his feet and patted him on the back. "Head to the hall Akio, I'm sure Yolanda will show you the way. This is only our first stop. We'll be moving on after breakfast." Akio and Yolanda left the room, Akio stopped and turned.

"Just one thing Raven. Why did the king refer to me as late? If you were here before?"

"There is only one in Danathor who knows who I am. Teju thought it best that we protect them that way," said Raven, saddened by the lie that had gone on for years. Akio sensed the tenderness of the subject and head off catching up with Yolanda. Raven stayed and looked on. He had never had the chance to hold what he should. It was not him who would one day call them his own. He turned and then left the room. On entering the hall he saw Akio eating with the king, Yolanda sitting next to them. He sat down himself and filled a plate.

"Eat up Akio, the journey is long," said Raven biting at his food. Akio nodded his head and continued eating. Raven noticed something. Yolanda hadn't broken her gaze on Akio since he had walked in the room. Could this be what was different? When Raven was last here as a young man, Yolanda was just a child. But Akio was now the same age. Strange.

Finishing his breakfast, Raven motioned to Akio who pushed his plate forward and stood up.

"Thank you for your hospitality Sire, but we must be off. I have given you the information you need. We will send word as soon as we know it," said Raven. "I do, however have one small request. Would the king be so kind as to lend two travelers horses to aid their journey?" The king looked confused.

"Raven, why is it you don't use magic?" Raven looked at Yolanda and the servants. The king then noticed it must be a private matter and asked them to leave. When they had gone Raven leant in and started to whisper.

"The use of magic notifies Raphael on our position. He would send creatures to kill Akio and myself in an instant. Wherever we are becomes a very dangerous place to be. Which is why I thank you so much again for keeping us for the night and why we are leaving so quickly." Raven turned to Akio. "Time to go."

Back in the underworld Raphael was pacing, most frustrated. Vigo ran into the room.

"My apologies, Raphael." Raphael strode up to him and hit him with the back of his hand knocking him to the floor.

"I will not miss this opportunity. I felt a rush of energy. They have reached Danathor. If the boy learns how to wield that sword and shield, then they will gain an advantage," said Raphael, leaning over Vigo's fallen body. "I do however have an edge. Something is different this time. I can't believe I almost missed it. Ready some dark walkers and send them to Danathor. We strike first." Vigo stood and went to run out of the room. Raphael smirked and a huge smile came across his face. "No, wait. Send them to Skye city and give them transport. I expect the old man is on his way there now." Vigo looked puzzled.

"To Skye city?"

"Yes, you stupid fool. If we attack the city they will be forced to go back. It gives us more time." He laughed in a maniacal, scheming way.

Meanwhile, Raven and Akio had left Danathor, and, now on horses were making better time. The sky was darker the closer they got. The feeling of pressure came over Akio and he started to fidget on his horse.

"What's wrong, Akio, you're forgetting I know what it means when you fidget like that. You can't get anything past yourself." He laughed.

"You said to trust my feelings right?" said Akio with a slight tremor in his voice.

"I did, your feelings are strong, trust them." Akio dipped into his pocket and pulled out the map.

"I feel something is wrong, but the map does nothing new, its shows the places I have been, but nothing's different. Wouldn't the map show it?" He said, handing the map to Raven. Just as Akio had said, all the places he had been were on the map, all still the same as when they first appeared. But Raven could see that Akio was bothered by something.

"We shall stop here for now and find some food. I'm not sure what it is you feel, but you may be right."

On the high winds Tiny flew ever on towards Skye city with Teju on his back. As they flew close to the outskirts Tiny began to drop a little.

"Hold on my friend. Soon enough we shall be there and you can have another rest, I know you're not used to this form or even flying as far as you have."

A few minutes later they saw the outskirts of Skye city. But what they saw was not expected. Somehow evil had found its way here first and was camped near the wooden log fence.

"Fly with haste Tiny. We must reach Mrs. Fritter and Mr. Yama as soon as we can."

Tiny Swooped down over the rooftops of outer Skye city and picked up speed. Finally they saw Mrs. Fritter's Inn. Tiny put his wings out and came to a stop slowly landing near the door. Teju jumped off and put Tiny back to normal.

"Rest my friend. You deserve it." Tiny hopped up onto Teju's hand, who put him in his coat pocket. He knocked frantically on the door. "Mrs. Fritter! You must open up!" he shouted.

"Alright, okay," said a muffled voice from behind the door. "Dear me, what is it?" asked Mrs. Fritter opening the door. "Bless my soul. It's you. You've come down from the mountain." Her face was struck with worry. She knew that something must be very wrong for him to come down after so many years. "You had better come in," she said standing aside.

"I'm afraid there's no time. Where is Mr. Yama? We must make use of his postal service. The War has started." Mrs. Fritter grabbed a big coat and headed out with Teju. They both hopped onto a pushbike leant against the sidewall and started off for Yama's Post.

"What is it you know? When will they arrive here?" shouted Mrs. Fritter back to Teju.

"The enemy has already moved. They have reacted quicker this time. In a matter of days Raphael's message will reach these boarders and creature will choose sides. After that, they will attack." replied Teju making sure Tiny was ok in his pocket.

"What must we do?" asked Mrs. Fritter.

"We must send letters to every man, woman and child in Skye City urging them to prepare. They will all need directions to the underground keep." Finally after a while they got to Yama's Post. Bursting in, Teju stumbled straight up to the desk. "It is time, my friend. The letters must be sent." Mr. Yama nodded and set the plan in motion.

"You mean you've known, this whole time? You knew this would happen?" Mrs. Fritter asked Mr. Yama. The magic postal gloves were working overtime sealing letter after letter.

"No. I was just prepared for if such an event. Teju believed so strongly in the prophecy it would not have boded well to ignore it completely. I was left instructions and followed through. I'm sorry I never told you," he said taking Mrs. Fritter's hands in his own. Teju looked out the window.

"I imagine we have three, maybe four days before word reaches Skye City." He turned around to Mr. Yama and Mrs. Fritter. "We must have as many people as possible underground before then. There is no more that we can do than that."

Back on the road, Akio and Raven had filled up on food and had returned to walking.

"Where are we headed now?" Akio asked.

"We make for the City of Moskai. It is raised off the ground, away from harm." Raven lowered his head. "Some harm anyway." Akio left it at that and sat back on his horse. After walking through the night they arrived at a big stone archway filled with swirls and lines.

"What's that?" asked Akio. Raven got off his horse and took hold of the reigns. Akio did likewise.

"That is the entrance to Moskai my friend. It's a portal for up there," said Raven, pointing up at a City high above them in the clouds. Akio looked up and saw a small glimpse of what looked like buildings. A City in the Sky in a world that's start was a City in the Sky. He was learning to accept that anything was possible. Raven stepped up to the portal. But nothing happened. He wondered what might be wrong. He looked back.

"Akio you try." He said. Akio stepped forward and into the Portal. But again nothing happened. "Something's wrong. This isn't right." Raven placed his staff on the rock and closed his eyes. The stone began to glow as the portal turned to a blue colour. "Step inside Akio, I will follow." Akio stepped through and came out up into the City, but there was not the sight waiting for him he had thought. Raven came through after and his face dropped instantly. Moskai had been completely destroyed. No people were left and all the buildings had been reduced to rubble. Raven walked up to a small pile and picked up a piece of rock. "They got here first." He then suddenly realized something. "Akio, take out your map," he said quickly. Akio dug into his pocket and took out the folded paper handing it to Raven. He opened it up and lay in out on the ground. Moskai appeared in ruin on the map; he moved his finger along it and muttered to himself. Raven had figured out their plan. "They are going to Skye City. They are trying to force us to go back. He knows we are on the move." He then folded the map and walked back over to the portal. "There's nothing we can do here Akio. We must press on." Akio was in shock. He grabbed Raven's coat and swung him round.

"Press on? Skye City is their target. Mr. Yama, Mrs. Fritter, all those people. We have to go back." Raven pulled away.

"And what do you suppose two of us do against whatever force has been sent? We need allies, but more so it is up to us to make sure this doesn't happen to as many people as possible. Teju has a plan in place. He's been waiting for you for 11 years, Akio. Now, we must get going." Raven went back through the portal followed by Akio.

"I'm sorry, Raven. I shouldn't have questioned you. You've been here a lot longer than I have. I should have trusted myself." Raven put his hand on Akio's shoulder and let out a sigh.

"No, you were right to react on your thoughts. You weren't to know that Teju had a plan and your protective nature took over." Back through the portal, Raven took his staff off the horse and let it run free; he took Akio's horse and let it free also. "One thing is for sure. We must quicken our pace even if it means using magic. He already knows we're coming. The enemy is further ahead than we thought. We are much deeper in than it seemed." Raven closed his cloak and crouched down. "Akio. Crouch and push all of your energy behind you. We fly for the mountain pass of Gresh to see the monks." Akio did as instructed, not sure if it would work. But to his amazement, he shot up into the air. Raven closely followed, shouting,

"Keep your energy under and behind you and push through. Concentrate, Akio, it will keep you in the air." He then shot off ahead. Akio closed his eyes and concentrated for a second. When he opened his eyes he was close behind. The feeling was like no other Akio had ever felt. The wind rushing past, birds should only feel the sense of freedom that he felt. This was brilliant.

Back in Skye City, everybody was making for the entrance to the underground keep. Tiny was flying around looking at all the people. Mr. Yama and Mrs. Fritter were at the main door directing people as they came. Teju was nearby standing on a stone looking out over the City. He thought of Akio and Raven and wondered how far they had gotten. He jumped down and called for Tiny to land in his hand. When he did Teju gave him a pat on the head.

"Do not worry, little one. I'm sure they are okay. They will come back." He then went over and joined the others, helping people into the underground.

Meanwhile deep in the underworld, sat on his throne, Raphael had sensed the surge of magic.

"I knew they would quicken their speed. The boy is learning quickly. He is taking to this world much better than I had thought. No matter." He sat up in his throne and tried to close in on their position. He looked inside his mind. "They are headed to the mountain of Gresh. So, it's the help of the dragons they seek. Then I shall do the same." He stood up and called for Vigo, who came running in and knelt at Raphael's feet. "Get up, you fool there is time wasting. They seek the help of the dragons, so we must find a force of equal strength." Vigo stood up and made a suggestion.

"We could send a scout of our own to the Fangol Gorge. There are dragons there that were previously banished for their ill thoughts and thievery. They have not re-serviced since." Raphael grabbed hold of Vigo excitedly.

"Yes! You're right. Those dragons still have a score to settle, they will surely want a chance at revenge." He let go of Vigo and pushed him backward. "See it done, Vigo. Recruit the dragons of the banished lands." Who then bowed to Raphael and left the room. "If they will not go back straight away, I will force them back."

The mountain of Gresh was in sight for the two travelers. They made their way upward and landed at an opening in the rock near to the top. Two big metal doors were imbedded in the mountain with markings all the way down. Raven re-set himself and stepped forward to the doors.

"This is the door to the monks holy temple. They traveled here long ago to try and learn the ways of the ancient dragon race. They will ask the dragon lord Lazarus for aid in dark times." Raven took up his staff and banged on the door. The door slowly opened and they both went in. They walked down long corridor deep into the mountain and came to a central chamber. There were monks scattered around chanting the ancient language of the spirits. One approached them.

"My sons, we have awaited your arrival. We have foreseen the reason you are here and await the answer from the dragon lord Lazarus. While you wait let us offer you beds for rest and food for your strength." He led them down another corridor into a small round room with two beds and a tray of food. "Eat, rest. You will have your answer soon." The monk then left the room and closed the door behind him. Raven walked up to the tray and took some food, which he took over to his bed.

"Get some rest Akio," he said lying down. "It seems they are prepared." Akio walked over and lay on the other bed and turned to Raven.

"Do you think they are okay?" he asked. Raven opened his eyes and turned his head to Akio.

"What does your heart tell you?" he asked. Akio pondered for a minute and then said.

"That we will have to go back." Raven took out the map from his pocket and threw it to Akio, who opened it up to reveal the mountain. He folded it back up and placed it in his pocket.

"When the time is right we will, Akio. If the dragons will help the message will be sent more quickly. For now they are safe." Raven turned back over to try and get some sleep. So Akio did the same.

About an hour past before there was a knock at the door. The same monk came in and got their attention.

"He wishes to give you his answer himself," he said to the both of them. "Come, follow me." Raven and Akio got up and followed the monk to a big opening in the mountain cave. The place started to shake and the wind picked up as, from below, up flew a huge horn-back dragon. He perched himself on the ledge and looked at Akio and Raven.

"You have come to claim aid from we dragons. I ask you, is this our war? When was the last time your kind helped us? We, who have stayed dormant in the mountains," bellowed Lazarus, in a booming voice that filled the mountain cave. Raven stepped forward.

"My lord Lazarus. This war will affect all kinds. It is time to unite. We ask for the aid of you, the mighty dragons. Men are foolish and fall to greed. But we alone cannot fight this. Please, will you help us? And you see the world renewed." Lazarus thought for a moment. He put his claw to his chin and then spoke once more.

"Long have we waited a new world. Where man and beast would bind together. I see you now come to honor that allegiance. You will have the power of the mountain dragons. We will set out on sending the message of war. Farewell for now." Lazarus flapped his big wings and flew out of the top of the mountain. He was then followed by a mass of dragons behind him. Raven had got the answer he wanted. It was now time to head for the edge of Hera. He turned to the monk and thanked him for his hospitality. There was no time to waste.

Over in the east, Vigo's scout had reached Fangol Gorge. It was a baron wasteland of soot and ash. Trees had been burned and a faint dust sat on the air. The scout made his way slowly through the trail, treading carefully as he went. The air was cold and silent. Just then with a horrendous thud a gigantic black dragon landed behind him and roared in his face.

"Who dare enter the borders of the banished dragon land?" He yelled, puffing his colossal chest. The scout cowered behind his shield and said with a worried voice,

"I have been sent by Raphael, lord of the underworld. He wishes you give him aid in the war of this world." The dragon gave a thunderous roar and moved his head a lot closer.

"And what would we receive should be grant such a request? The time has come, has it? We have waited here since banishment for a chance to reclaim our place. Tell me puny being, Why should we help, after being left here to gradually die out?"

"In return for your help, the great Raphael is willing to give you the land to the north; he can break your bindings to this place," replied the scout, poking his head out from behind the shield. This offer intrigued the dragon. The magic that kept them in the Gorge could be broken and they would once again be free to roam as they wished.

"Tell your master that we accept his offer. I am Roaga, master of the black dragons. I give him my word. Now leave this place. You will see us again soon." Roaga then took to the sky blowing dust and ash all over. Still terrified, the scout hastily made his way out of the Gorge. The two sides were taking shape.

Akio and Raven had reached the dark sky of the northern border. They flew fast over the trees of the Cullen forest. Soon enough the gates of Hera were in sight. They flew up and over the wall and landed on the market road. A soldier ran over and extended his arm to Raven.

"It is good to see you. I guess with your return we know what it means. We received Teju's letter," he said. "But I'm afraid I have bad news. Since you have been away, the king has passed, and with no son command of Hera fell to Bogal, captain of the northern army. I will take you to him now." They went up the road and across the town, upstairs and into the great hall of Hera before reaching the throne room. There was Bogal leaning over a table instructing others. He looked up and saw Raven and Akio. He came over and shook their hands.

"Akio, we have our army ready and have made plans for a legion to join you as well," he said to Raven. He looked at Akio. "Ah you must be the other. I suppose you're Akio now." He turned back to Raven. "I shall refer to you as others do, Raven. Come." Bogal went back over to the table and continued to consult the map. Akio tapped on Raven's shoulder.

"He knows who you are?"

"When I was young, I stayed here for a while. Bogal and I became good friends. He is one of few who knows who I really am." Akio nodded in acceptance and they both then went over and joined them at the table. "Raphael has sent a movement to strike on Skye City. He means to push Akio and myself back," said Raven. "We need to take our legion with us back to the City. You must hold here. We will return to Danathor and request that they send soldiers to join you." Akio had been quiet a while, but an idea sparked in his head.

"Why not lure them out?" he said to the other two. Raven and Bogal looked at each other and turned to Akio.

"To where, and why my boy?" asked Bogal, confused. Akio stepped forward to the table and began to explain his plan.

"All this time we have kept passing each other. After a while all will see a similar fate to Moskai. We are trying to avoid a battle that is going to happen no matter how long we put it off." He turned to Raven. "It's like you said, it's unavoidable. We either try to run forever, or we finally put it right." Raven smiled and placed his hand on Akio. He was right, it was time to do something.

"Bogal, ready our soldiers. It's time to go back." Said Raven. "Akio, we shall eat to regain our strength and then it's off back to Danathor. It is a long way and we'll have to continue through night and day." Akio and Raven then made their way into the dining hall as servants put out food on the tables. They each sat down and began to eat. As they did, Bogal came through. "We will need to visit your armory, Bogal. Magic can do so much, but sometimes the cold blade of a sword and a trusty shield is needed," said Raven. Bogal nodded and signaled to a servant to open the doors. Raven stood up and gestured for Akio to follow. They walked in to a room filled with swords, shields, catapults, armor and other such weapons of war.

"Pick out some weapons Akio, as light as possible," said Raven, picking up a sword and testing it out. Akio walked around looking at all there was. Then over in a corner he saw a long sword in a back sheath. He pulled out the sword and swung it to test the weight. It was surprisingly light and seemed strong. He strapped it on his back and started looking for a small dagger. Raven had finished deciding and came over, holding a dagger he gave to Akio.

"This is made from Iridium. It will serve you well." Akio took the dagger and strapped it to his waist. As they made their way back outside, the soldiers were waiting. Time to go back.

Chapter 5

Back To Move Forward

It would take a long time for the army to make its way all the way to Danathor, so a better plan was needed. The longer they took, the more ground the dark army gained on them. Raven knew he had the power to transport them all instantly, but was afraid of what would happen. Raphael already knew their position so using magic wasn't an issue. But the amount of power it would take would drain him completely and risked bringing him near death. But time was wasting and it didn't seem like there was any other option.

"Akio, I can transport us all back to Danathor in a matter of seconds. But there is one problem. Using such power will bring me near to death but I see no other way of not wasting any more time. The enemy is constantly moving. A lot quicker than I could have imagined." He handed Akio a vile of glowing liquid. "When we arrive you must give this to me instantly. You will have to make sure I swallow it as I will not be conscious and won't be for a while." Raven went up to Bogal and said his goodbyes. "You will be safe for now. Akio and myself are their targets, but stay sharp and watch the horizon, we must defend Skye City and lands between. Hopefully we shall return." He then told everyone in the army to join hands and then take hold of Akio. Raven then took hold of Akio's hand and said, "When the aura is strong, take a breath." He closed his eyes and concentrated hard. The wind picked up and surges of energy grazed over his body. He let out a scream and a red aura surrounded the group. Akio took a breath and whoosh. They were transported to the centre of Danathor all falling to the ground. Akio couldn't believe that they were back so quickly. He then remembered what Raven had said. He ran over to see

Raven lying on the floor. He was completely motionless. Akio rushed and took out the vile and poured it into Raven mouth. Nothing seemed to happen until Raven moved his fingers.

Garron and Yolanda ran over.

"Take him to a bed and make sure he is looked after," shouted Garron to some nearby subjects. The army from Hera had gathered round and parted to make way for them to take Raven through. Garron shook Akio's hand and looked at the army. "It is time to combine then. There is much to discuss." Akio walked in with Garron and through into the throne room. Yolanda looked on, not taking her eyes of Akio.

"There is not a lot of time, Garron," said Akio. "The enemy has moved to strike Skye City, they mean to force Raven and myself back. They will no doubt pass here but they mean not to attack here yet." Garron sat on his throne as a chair was brought for Akio. "Raven will need rest, but when he is ready we must head off again. I'm sorry we can't stay long." Garron nodded.

That night Akio was with Norx at the tower gate. It was quiet but there was an ill feeling in the air.

"Will you be leaving in the morning?" asked Norx.

"I expect so, my friend. We have to get back to Skye City," replied Akio. "Although I don't really know how. Walking will take a couple of days, but for Raven to do the same spell again, he will be weakened once again." Norx thought for a moment and then said,

"If you were the same person, you could combine your powers together. That way it wouldn't be so dangerous, right?" He was right. All this time Akio had been leaving Raven to do most of the magic. But he could help. That way they could transport everyone back to Skye City in the morning.

Raven woke to Akio sitting at his bedside. He sat up.

"Welcome back. How do you feel?" asked Akio. Raven spun round and sat next to Akio.

"I'm okay. A little faint but it will pass. Did you explain the plan to Garron?"

"Yes, he knows. But I was thinking. That last trip took a lot out of you. If we were to combine our strength, we could travel quickly back to Skye City. If you'd show me how to do it." Raven stood up and pulled his hood on.

"It is probably the best option. I don't know why I didn't think of that before. They must be getting close to the City. There is no time to waste." They left the room and headed for the courtyard. Outside the army was waiting with Garron and Yolanda waiting too. Raven walked up to Garron and thanked him once again for keeping them.

"I thank you again, my friend. Even if I spent most of it laid out," Raven said to Garron. Akio went over to Yolanda.

"Again it seems we have been given short time," she said to Akio.

"There will be time. I'd ask for you to come with us but it will be too dangerous for you there. You have to prepare for what is to come. If they can't take Skye City, they will surely come here next. Goodbye Yolanda."

Akio and Raven joined the army who had been increased by those from Danathor, there was now close to 100 of them. They all joined hands and took hold of Akio and Raven.

"Now concentrate on your destination, Akio and let the energy fill you up," said Raven. "Concentrate hard and when the time feels right let it all out. Don't forget to take a breath." Raven and Akio closed their eyes and concentrated on the market town in Skye City. Once again the wind picked up and the aura appeared. In a flash of red light they disappeared and were transported to Skye City. On arrival Akio fell to the floor. His head was muffled and he was incredibly dizzy. He tried to stand but the first few attempts failed. On the third time Raven took his arm and pulled him up.

"Well done, Akio. Well done indeed, that was very good for your first time. And don't worry, the feeling will fade." Akio shook his head and tried to gain his proper vision.

"You weren't affected this time?" he asked Raven who seemed to be normal.

"No it did, my energy is low, but with splitting it between the two of us it was not as big of a blow. This was your first time so it's normal to be affected this much." They looked around. The soldiers were all standing up and getting themselves together. But the city was like they had entered a ghost town. The army was now all on their feet and awaited instruction. Raven knew they would have made for the underground keep. It was just a matter of remembering where the entrance was. Teju had told him of this place and how to find it, but that had been a long time ago and he couldn't remember.

"Akio, pass me the map." Akio took the map from his pocket and handed it to Raven. He took it from him and opened it up. All the places appeared and Raven waved his hand over the position of Skye City. The image on the map seemed to grow as if going inside the City on the map. The map now showed Skye City in more detail across the whole map.

"It did that before, just the other way," said Akio. Raven looked at the map and saw the statue rock that Teju had spoken about.

"This way," shouted Raven who started to head off down the road. Akio and the army followed behind as Raven followed the map. They came to an enormous stone statue on a King holding a scroll.

"This is it," said Raven to himself. He started banging his staff on the ground until he found a part that sounded hollow. He handed the map back to Akio and then held his staff up straight on the ground. He muttered a spell.

"Aprire per favore la porta alla sicurezza." The ground then began to shake and open. The grass and soil began to part from each other revealing a path heading underground.

"Come on," said Raven leading the group down the path. Down the pathway Akio looked at what was on the walls. All the way down were scriptures in different languages and pictures drawn of times past. It was like a long time line of this world. He saw a drawing of a boy that looked just like him. He stopped and looked at it for a second. He noticed he was now a little behind, so carried on down the path. After a while they finally saw people. Teju stood up when he saw Raven. With glee he ran up and they embraced.

"Raven. I knew you would return." Tiny flew off Teju's shoulder and bowled into Akio's arms. Teju turned to Akio. "This one has missed you a lot, my boy." Tiny was chirping with happiness at seeing Akio. It had been a while since they had seen each other.

"We have brought forces from Hera and Danathor. But I am afraid they are few," said Raven to Teju. Mrs. Fritter and Mr. Yama came over and both gave a big hug to Akio.

"We are so glad to see you," said Mr. Yama. Raven came over to them and took down his hood.

"Mr. Yama, Mrs. Fritter. It is nice to finally meet you properly. We didn't really meet the first time." Mrs. Fritter came over and looked Raven up and down. She was hesitant at first. She looked at Akio, and then back at Raven, looking at his eyes. Innocence developed in Raven's eyes, a sight Akio had only seen once before when Raven had first seen Tiny. In that moment Mrs. Fritter recognised the man that stood before her.

"It is you, but a lot older." She gave him a big hug. "It's okay my sweet." She let him go and he turned to Mr. Yama. He too saw that he was just an older version of Akio.

"Now, I suspect that the first of the dark army will be here by morning. No matter what happens, stay below," said Raven to the three of them. Akio and Tiny went and sat together. It was good to see everyone again.

Through the night they all spoke and swapped stories of the last year. They spoke of what happened, what was to come, and what they could do if the war was won.

"Will you be using Tiny tomorrow?" asked Teju. Akio looked at Tiny, who hopped up ready to go.

"It would seem he wants to be there with me," laughed Akio, stroking Tiny's head.

"We should try and get some sleep. We will be going back out in the morning," said Raven, heading to a bed and lying down. Akio agreed and made his way to his own bed. He lay his head down. He had portrayed a strong outer image, but inside he was frightened. Tomorrow was the start of something much bigger. Over the past year Akio had grown from a boy in a new world to a confident young man, but what was to come was still very overwhelming.

All too soon for Akio, the morning came. Raven and Akio armoured up and after saying farewell to the others, lead the army up the path to above. They walked into the centre of the town and from over the hill came a hoard of rogues, Cyclops, un-dead and men who had sought out power, with evil in their hearts.

"Ready!" shouted Raven to the army who all banged their shields in reply. "Ready yourself, Akio. This is it. Show no mercy." The enemy got closer and closer. Raven lifted his sword in the air waiting to give the signal to charge. Akio put Tiny in his big form and jumped on his back. The suspense and tension grew and Akio's breathing increased. They all stood waiting until Raven shouted.

"Now!" Everyone ran forward charging the dark army. Akio and Tiny took to the sky flying over to the mass of creatures charging down the hill. The two forces collided, clashing swords and armour. Akio and Tiny swooped down connecting swords with those below. Raven shot out spell after spell knocking creatures back. He blocked with his sword, and stabbed another. He looked up.

"Akio look out!" he yelled as a black dragon flew into sight heading straight for Akio and Tiny. They avoided the collision with milliseconds to spare. They circled round, and Akio shot a flame at the dragon who swerved away.

Down on the ground Raven was jumping and running through the mass of bodies piling up. He forced his staff into the ground and flung himself forward, holding his sword out straight. He landed blocked, stabbed and avoided. More black dragons came and surrounded Akio and Tiny. What to do now? They charged but before they got to them, the dragons of the mountain came flying to Akio's aid. Tiny dipped down and away from danger. But it would only be for a second as a group of rogues had rolled up a catapult. They placed big rocks inside and flung them through the air. Tiny did well to avoid the first ones, but in avoiding a black dragon, one of the rocks hit. He fell from the sky and crashed down with Akio creating a big thud. Akio was thrown from Tiny's back. He quickly got up and ran over.

"Tiny?" he said worryingly. "Tiny?" He shook him hard to try and revive him. Tiny was hurt. He barely opened an eye and made a small whimpering sound. Akio grew angry. He turned to see a bunch of rogues closing in. Akio screamed in anger, releasing a wave of energy knocking them all back. He turned Tiny back to his smaller size and hid him under cover.

"I'll come back, don't worry," he told Tiny. He then ran into the battle. He joined Raven and the both of them turned and fought back to back. Dragons were falling from the sky from both sides, injured or even killed. A troll thudded his way over and knocked Raven away. He went to swing his club at Akio, who avoided the first swing but did not avoid the second. Akio was tossed through the air, landing on a fallen black dragon. Raven ran back in releasing a freezing spell from his staff, sticking the troll's arm to the ground. He chopped down with his sword and then struck again, cutting the troll's arm clean off. Akio got up and ran to help. As Raven chopped at the trolls leg Akio jumped on his other arm. He swung at the Troll's head burying his sword deep into the flesh. He jumped off and both Raven and Akio stuck their swords into the troll's chest. It fell down dead. Once again they went back to back continuing with the fight. Akio lifted a shield from the ground and blocked a blow. He then threw the shield at a Cyclops, hitting it in its eye. The Cyclops yelled in pain and ran off into the distance.

"Akio, make a fire ring," shouted Raven. They both made fire in their hands and started to spin. Lots of the enemy caught fire and ran from the battlefield. They stopped and split. Akio ran to help some soldiers as Raven flew through the air taking out some foes. Akio then came one on one with a rogue on a horse. He galloped forward swinging at Akio, who blocked and turned, but not quick enough as on return the rider cut Akio's arm. Akio dropped to a knee, clutching his arm. On seeing this Raven ran over and took the rider off his horse and pushing his sword into its chest. He pulled Akio to his feet.

"Put your hands next to mine," said Raven. "Strong energy now!" he shouted. Akio did as asked, combining his strength with Raven's. It shot out over the battlefield throwing the enemy back. It was almost over.

"Just a little more, Akio." Another rogue ran over to Raven and Akio, but from out of his cover Tiny made a dash at him knocking him over. He swatted Tiny away hitting him into a fallen tree. Akio took up his sword and took off the rouges head. The dragons of the mountain had seen off those from the banished lands and with that the dark army went into retreat.

"Fall back!" shouted Raven. "Save your strength. This is only but a blip of what is to come." Akio ran over to Tiny. He picked him up off the ground. Raven ran over and knelt at Akio's side. Tiny wasn't moving, not even his little chest. A tear rolled down Akio's face. Tiny had died.

"No. No!" Akio screamed, at the top of his voice. Raven got Akio to his feet still cradling Tiny in his hands. They made their way back into the underground keep. Less than half of them returned. Teju, Mrs. Fritter and Mr. Yama saw Akio and Raven walking back over. They saw

Tiny in Akio's hands and their hearts dropped. Mrs. Fritter hurried over and put her arms around Akio. Teju came over with a piece of cloth and string and strapped up Akio's arm. He looked down at Tiny in his hands. He had lost his dearest and first friend in this world who had been with him from the very start.

Back in the underworld, Raphael was plotting his next move.

"That was merely a start," he said to Vigo. "Send more and send them to Danathor this time. If I can get my hands on that fool Michael's sword, I can end this war much sooner than intended." He went over to a layout of the land sat on a table. "Skye City matters little to me. That was just to draw them back. We now destroy our way back here, taking each kingdom as we go." He laughed.

Back in Skye City, Mr. Yama had found a small box to use for Tiny's burial. Akio placed Tiny inside and put the box in a hole. Raven then filled the hole and created a small gravestone at the head.

"You were my first friend here Tiny. I will miss you little one," said Akio kneeling at the grave. Mr. Yama and Raven placed their hands on Akio's shoulders to try and console him. Akio stood up and let out a big sigh. "Well, no time to stop I suppose. What's our next move, Raven?"

"There will be a time to grieve, Akio, but for now we will send what we have left to Danathor. I expect they will gradually make their way back to the underworld. But I do promise, a time *will* come to grieve," Raven said picking up his staff. Akio nodded and stood up.

Later on, the army was sent off while Raven and Akio stayed to help rebuild what was destroyed in the town. A message bird was sent to Danathor to warn of the impending threat. With just the two of them, transportation would be much easier.

Soon enough the time came and Akio and Raven would be on the move yet again. They said their goodbyes and got ready to transport themselves to Danathor. Akio laid a pile of birdseed on Tiny's grave and then he and Raven transported themselves back to Danathor. They landed in the courtyard and then made their way through into the throne room, to see Garron sitting near a window. He saw them come in and got up to greet them.

"Garron. You received my note?" said Raven embracing Garron. Garron shook Akio's hand.

"I did," he said to Raven. "How long do you think we have?"

"Maybe two days, they move with haste. What was left from Skye City closely follows them, but I assure you more will be sent." Garron nodded and they all made their way to inform the rest.

The City began to prepare. The gates were secured and the beacons were lit for war. Troops lined the City walls and gathered in the main courtyard. Archers were placed in towers and the women and children sealed deep within the castle. Every man and boy able to bear arms was provided with swords, shields and armour. Garron, Raven and Akio stood with Norx in the tower gate. By evening everything was ready for the imminent attack. Everybody slept at their post that night. The air was tense and an ill silence hung all around.

"Have you not slept?" asked Raven, walking up to Akio.

"No. I can't help but think of what is still to come. What just happened, I'd never been in a war before." Akio thought of home and how he had gotten here. It had been a long time, so much had happened. He thought of Tiny and when he first arrived. Meeting Mr. Yama, Mrs. Fritter and Teju. And now here he stood on the eve of another battle and no further it seemed to saving this world.

"You did so very well Akio, and I am proud of you. I know it's hard accepting all of this. But believe me, you're taking to it much better than I did." Raven laughed. The two then stayed silent and just stood appreciating the night.

The morning of the second day dawned and the city was racked with nerves. The sun could not be seen through the clouds and the rain fell hard. Garron walked up and down the city wall anxious for the enemies' arrival. But the sound of marching feet and horns did not come from the south. The sound came from the other side of the city. More had come from the underworld. Garron, Akio and Raven ran through the city to the northern wall. A sea of creatures lay before them. Fear struck the face of Garron.

"We cannot stand against such a force. We readied ourselves for the ones from the south, but not for more from the other side. The city, I fear, will fall," he said worriedly. Raven grabbed hold of him and tried to get some sense into him.

"You can't give up. So they have come from the north, we will still fight as hard. We stand with you Garron. We all do," said Raven clutching at the king's robes. Just then a sign of hope flew into view. More mountain dragons had come to help. They flew over the masses and took up position over the city walls. The dark army stopped just outside the northern gate. Through the crowd they rolled a battering ram with a troll at the far end. He took a step back, and then ran the ram at the gate. It crashed into the gate, but it did not give. He did so again, but again it did not give. Another troll came and stood behind the other and they both ran at the gate. The battering ram smashed through and the enemy flooded into the city. It had begun. Bodies collided. Swords clanged together, the trolls smashed more and more with their big clubs. Inside the castle the women and children could do nothing but listen to the horror that came from outside.

"Will they get through my lady?" a woman asked Yolanda, holding a small child in her arms. With a worried look on her face Yolanda answered,

"I don't know."

Outside the battle raged on and more of the city destroyed. Raven and Akio stood atop the wall firing as fast as they could. Then, coming up from the south the creatures that had attacked Skye city had arrived to join the fight. On seeing this, Garron pointed his sword and shouted.

"To the south. Troops to the south." Men ran for the south entrance, they tried to bolt the gates further but were knocked from it by a black dragon. Raven noticed that some were trying to get into the main doorway. Knowing he could not let them get through, he jumped from his position and stormed towards them. He threw a spell knocking them from the door and then proceeded to swing his sword violently. Akio saw and hurried to join him. The two took up their same position of back to back, swinging and stabbing as they went. But this time it was not as effective. Defeat seemed close, as they were outnumbered and losing numbers quickly. Raven leant back to Akio.

"We need to draw them out of the city. We are surrounded on all sides. We're trapped." Akio looked for an opening. But with so many around them, it seemed there wouldn't be a chance. He thought for a second. Surely they had been told of Raphael's plan. If so it would be Akio they would go after. Quickly, Akio leapt up onto a fallen part of the city.

"Creatures, beasts, men from the dark. I am the one you seek. I Akio, call for you to follow me," he shouted. All attention turned to him. He flew up into the air and flew out into the field. He landed and looked up. Sure enough, a whole section of the enemy turned and ran towards him.

"Akio, no!" screamed Raven. As many of them then ran towards Akio, Raven caught as many as he could. If Akio was killed the war could never be finished. He tried to get to Akio as fast as possible and took to the air. With seconds to spare he landed next to Akio and they collided with the enemy.

"To the fields!" ordered Garron leading troops out of the city. As they got back into battle, a ray of hope showed itself. The legion from Skye City had arrived. The mountain dragons took down the black dragons then turned their attention to the ground. Then in the distance, there was an encouraging sight. A glint of light reflected off the armour of Hera horsemen. Reinforcements had come. They rode fast through the north gate of the city, toppling foes as they went. They continued out into the fields and eased the tension. As nightfall came it seemed the tables had turned. With no black dragons left and all dark beings on foot, the Hera horsemen had a distinct advantage. Victory was in sight. The rain continued as horses and men fought against the muddy ground and energies were fading. It would have to be finished soon. Akio ran back into the city and made his way to where Michael's sword and shield were held. He came to an abrupt stop and slowly reached out to the weapons. But yet again he was denied the power of the weapons. He didn't understand. If they weren't needed now, when would they be? There was no time to think about it, so he got up and ran back outside to the battle. When he returned to the field the understanding was found. With the battle drawing to a close they wouldn't be needed. The sun began to rise and Raven came over leaving the Hera horsemen to fend off the rest.

"I know what you're thinking Akio. They are not needed, as this is not all we will see. Raphael will not send all his might at once, that isn't his plan." Akio sheathed his sword and sat on the step.

"What is his plan?" he asked. Raven perched himself next to Akio and lay his staff on the ground.

"Raphael means to kill you Akio. He will do all he can to achieve that. But he knows something. And I suspect he has known for a while."

"What's that?" asked Akio. Raven looked up at the sky.

"Michael was never killed. He knows that when the time is right he will return. He will not use up all of his force at once for fear if he does, he will be left defenceless and Michael will make his move. Unless..." Garron walked up and informed them of the victory.

"Walls will need to be rebuilt and the dead disposed of properly," he said. "But I have a feeling you won't be staying long." Raven stood up and took Garron's forearm.

"We will have some time. Raphael will strike again. But will need to regroup." Akio stood too and went over to the main door of the castle where men were taking the barricade down. They opened the doors and the women and children made their way out. People embraced and took a look at the destruction that had happened. Others consoled ones who had lost loved ones in the fight. Garron stepped up high and addressed the people.

"While we mourn our brothers who fought and fell, we remember what it was they fought for. Walls can be built. But that does not make a kingdom. Monuments can stand tall. But they do not replace those who they mean to honour. Those who give themselves to the fight of freedom, make a kingdom. Men who draw swords that tremble in their hands earn their place in our hearts. That is how we honour them. Tonight we will pay homage to those who fell in battle. A feast for the fallen!" The people cheered. Raven went up to Garron.

"A speech well made, my friend. Tonight we enjoy what small bout of peace this city has found."

That night in the great hall, a magnificent feast took place. People danced and ate, drank and laughed. Akio watched as Yolanda danced. As he did, time slowed, and all other distractions filtered from his mind. A small flutter touched his heart and a small smile was brought to his face. King Garron stood and called for people's attention.

"We raise our goblets, not to Danathor, but those who fought and died to defend it. Hail!"

"Hail!" they all shouted. Akio bowed his head to the king and raised his goblet, before making his way out to a balcony. Raven saw this and followed him out. Akio was leaning on the ledge looking up at the stars.

"You know. Some say that warriors that fall in battle take to the sky to keep watch on those who follow them. The ones that shine brightest are the new arrivals and will find a way to settle." They stood silently for a second. "He's up there somewhere, Akio."

Who's that?" asked Akio.

"My Tiny. And yours," replied Raven. The thought then dropped. If Akio had a Chika bird, Raven would have had one too.

"That's why there was a bond the first time you saw Tiny. Was it the same? No, it couldn't have been. The timeline has changed." Raven let out a sigh of sadness.

"Teju had hid me from the world. Over the years I learned to fight and wield powerful magic, with Tiny by my side. Soon enough Raphael learned I had come. Teju tried to keep me hidden staying for periods of time in different places. Until I thought it was time to see what it was I was hiding from. I used the transport spell, but as you know now, which I didn't back then, Raphael can sense strong surges of magic. He knew I was coming before I even arrived. As soon as I landed he was waiting. The blast almost killed me, and Raphael thought it had. My Tiny was not as lucky as I was that day. I stumbled from the gates of the underworld and wandered for days with Tiny in my arms. My energy ran out and I collapsed for dead. If Teju hadn't have followed me and found me, I wouldn't be here. I never ventured that far north again." Akio put his arm on Raven as a tear rolled down his face. "I'm sorry you lost your friend as well, Akio." Akio leant back on the ledge.

"So much death. So much affected by our coming. Are we even meant to be here?" asked Akio, almost irritated by his arrival in this world. Raven turned to him and placed his hands on his shoulders.

"Yes Akio. Time sent us here, not once, but twice. There is something we must finish. I was foolish before. We thought it was over, that we had failed. But then you came and brought new light to our cause." Akio felt a sense of relief from Raven. He was right, there must be a reason he was sent here again. They both decided to rejoin the others inside. The night drew to a close, and people made their way to their homes. Akio and Raven started to make their way out of the great hall when Yolanda shouted after them.

"Akio." She made her way up and smiled at them both. "Akio, would you like to walk with me a while before we retire for the night?" she asked. Akio looked at Raven who gestured for him to go.

"That would be nice," Akio said. So they walked down the corridor and outside together. They walked through the gardens. Much of it had been affected by the battle. Yolanda crouched down and picked up a flower that had been pulled from the ground.

"Such beauty trampled on by evil," she said as she stood. Akio walked over and took the flower and placed it in her hair.

"Sometimes, when you still believe in something. Or even if it seems all hope has been lost and has been stolen from you. All you have to do is look at it differently. And beauty will still shine through," he said. Yolanda took Akio's hands and looked him in the eye.

"I feel I know you. Like I have seen you in my dreams. And yet, still a mystery. A hero from another world comes to our aid." She pulled away and turned to face away. "But I can't get attached. Because one day you will leave." Akio went to touch her, but she flinched away.

"I feel it too, but you won't let me near. I don't know what my future holds. I didn't know I would be here now. But whatever happens, I will be there. I promise you. And if the time comes where I have to leave. I will promise you one more thing." Akio turned her around and looked at her. "I will come back." A tear of joy trickled down Yolanda's cheek and she jumped into Akio's arms. Akio spun round clutching Yolanda and his heart filled with warmth. From up in his chamber Garron looked on.

"A hero comes, and gives a world his life. And brings a smile long awaited by a father who thought it would never come. I rest happy tonight," he muttered to himself, who then retired to his bed. Akio came into his and Ravens sleeping quarters and lay on his bed. Raven was asleep. He lay there with his eyes open for a while. He smiled and then rolled over to get some sleep. In a world it seemed that was ravished by darkness, he felt a glimmer of light in his heart. There would be a lot to do tomorrow, so he thought it best he tried to sleep.

At day break. Akio and Raven, along with many others had started to clear up the mess from the battle. With Akio and Raven using mostly magic, it was easier to clear the rubble. Yolanda came out and smiled at Akio, who smiled back.

"So, you've made quite the impression on the young princess Akio," said Raven clearing some rubble. Akio stopped and looked at Raven.

"If we end this. I'll have to go back won't I?" said Akio, disappointed.

"Yes." Said Raven. "Even if you stayed, there would come a time where you'd have to go back. But you will always remember and be remembered here. But don't think about that now." Raven went back to clearing the city while Akio walked over to Yolanda.

"May we walk for a while?" he asked her. She nodded and they walked off together. All over the city people where clearing and re building.

"I know once this is over, I will have to go back to where I came from. But that doesn't stop the way I feel." He turned to Yolanda who looked longingly into her eyes. "But no matter where we are, I know I will be thinking of you. Since I've been here, so much has happened. Things like this don't happen every day." He laughed. "Just over a year ago I was in a new city going for a look around with my friend, only to be whisked off to a world I never knew existed. And now I've met you and I feel even stranger than when I got off that train." But before he could finish, an injured smaller black dragon flew over the wall and took hold of Yolanda. Akio was thrown aside and the dragon made off with the young princess.

"Yolanda!" Akio shouted. He got up and ran fast into the courtyard yelling as he went. "Yolanda. Yolanda has been taken." Raven and Garron hurried their way to meet

Akio. "We have to go after her." puffed Akio. Raven looked at Garron, and then back at Akio.

"Come on, let's go."

Chapter 6

New Will

Raven and Akio hurried to their quarters and suited up ready to go. Garron appeared at the doorway.

"Will you need any men?" He asked Raven.

"Send them to the east and west. Seek help from the Elves of the Whitewood forest and the Elvor of the eastern shore. Then march on the gates of the underworld. It seems Lord Raphael's plans have changed." Raven tightened his belt, then he and Akio headed for the northern gate.

"We will transport to the Black fields outside the underworld gates. He will know we have come, but it seems it is what he wants. We will make our way in slowly and try to avoid any confrontation." said Raven to Akio following close behind. Garron grabbed Raven's arm and pulled him back.

"Bring her back to me." Raven shook Garron's hand to reassure him.

"We will get her back." Raven and Akio then left Danathor and transported themselves to the black fields.

As expected there was no one waiting. Raphael clearly wanted them to find their way in. Like he was beckoning them. Slightly crouched, they made their way slowly through the fields. The ground was soot and the sky was black. A cold chill filled the air. Akio had tried to imagine what it would look like this far north. Raven put his finger to his lips, gesturing for Akio to stay quiet. He then whispered, "You will find no more dangerous place Akio. We must do our best not to be seen. If we are, you can be certain they will kill us where we stand. Especially you." He slowly turned back around and signalled for Akio to follow him. Rogues, Harpies and goblins wandered the space around the gate. They would have to find another way in. Raven looked around and noticed a mound of skulls piled by a nearby wall. He pointed to Akio and they both slowly made their way over. Raven placed a foot on the pile. Some rolled down and made a small sound. He quickly lifted his foot and tried to place it again more carefully. They could not fly up. The use of magic this close would reveal their position straight away and they would surely be ambushed. When Raven had made some progress up the mound, Akio followed behind him. They hopped over the wall and slid down the other side. The danger had grown; they were now in the kingdom of the underworld.

All the way back in Skye City, Mr. Yama and Mrs Fritter were looking for Teju. They hadn't seen him for about an hour. They wandered down a small lane and over to Mrs Fritter's inn. They went in and looked in rooms to see if he was there. They found him in one of the rooms upstairs putting armour under a robe and lashing a sword to his waist.

"What are you doing?" asked Mr. Yama walking in the room.

"The first time I interfered and stopped the war from taking place. Now that time has set things back in motion, I have sent two men to solve a problem that I was a part of causing. It would not be right if I did not lend myself to the fight. Try to put things right." He then pulled up his hood and headed out the room. Mr. Yama and Mrs. Fritter followed him out.

"Teju, I know you think you are to blame. But you're not, you did what you thought was right. But if you go into battle, you will fall easier than you would have before. You're an older man now." Teju turned to the both of them.

"A measure of a man is not by days spent. It is what he does with those days that make him who he is. I knew this day would come. I now know what it is I have to do." Before they could reply, he had left the inn. Scared but sure, Teju made his way up the path and pulled out his wand. First he would go to Danathor and consult with the king. He closed his eyes and concentrated. It had been a while since he had used the transport spell and didn't even know if it would work. Slowly an aura appeared around him as he focused on the City centre. After a while of concentration he began to disappear. He then arrived in Danathor weakened by the spell he had not done for many years. A nearby Danthorian saw him arrive and pulled him up. He supported him into the castle, and took him to the throne room.

"My king." The Danthorian said. "This man just appeared in the courtyard. I brought him straight to you. He seems to be weak." Garron stepped down from his throne and helped support Teju.

"Teju. What are you doing here?" Teju lifted his head and said.

"I have come to support the warriors and to help Raven and Akio. This is as much my war as theirs." It was clear that Teju needed to rest. Garron motioned to two servants at the far wall who came and took Teju to a bed. Teju lay and relaxed himself.

"Bring some water," Garron said to one of the servants. "Try to rest Teju. We will speak when you have your strength back." Garron then left the room and let the servants tend to Teju.

Back in the underworld, Raven and Akio had remained unseen. They had made it to the east tower. They would have to climb their way up to a window. Raven tied his staff to his back and started up the wall. Akio followed and they both made their way up the wall and climbed in a small window. It was a small room with a door on the far side. Raven went slowly up to the door and placed his ear upon it. He couldn't hear anything so it was safe to open it and go through. They went down a long empty passage and spied a couple of rogues waiting by an archway. Raven picked up a small stone and through it to get their attention. The rouges heard the noise and went to investigate it. Raven and Akio quickly went under the arch and carried on through the dark fortress. Just then Akio felt a flutter in his chest. He stopped and closed his eyes. He could feel Yolanda's presence. He saw in his mind going down a corridor and into a big room. Yolanda was tied to a rock sticking out of the ground inside a big hole. Rouges, goblins men and wolves surrounded her. He opened his eyes and whispered to Raven.

"I can feel her Raven. I can find her." He tried to sense her again and began walking in the direction. Raven followed him looking for enemies as they went. He didn't like how easy this was. Where were the creatures of the underworld? Had they walked into a trap? They continued on and came to a long bridge over a pit of what looked like fire.

"Careful Akio. This is the pit of lost souls. Falling in doesn't only kill you. But your soul will belong to Raphael for all eternity." Akio looked over. It sure wasn't fire. Millions of souls flew lost in a sea of nothingness, all fighting to see what light they would never witness again. They then sank down never to be seen, only heard through the ongoing groans of those who were dead. Akio carefully lead the way across the bridge.

"Can you still feel her Akio? Trust your feelings." asked Raven.

"Yes. And it's getting stronger." He answered crossing the bridge. He stepped forward and a piece of the bridge broke away and fell into the pit. It started to crumble under Akio's feet. He scrambled back but was not quite quick enough.

"Akio!" shouted Raven rushing over. He slid on his front and looked over the edge. Luckily Akio had gotten hold of the side and was hanging on.

"I think that may have given us away," said Akio trying not to let go. Raven held out his hand and Akio tried to get hold.

"Come on," said Raven reaching as far as he could. With one last effort Akio grabbed Raven's hand and was pulled back onto the bridge. They both lay on the bridge for a second.

"That was close," said Akio. Raven sat up and heard a rustle coming towards them.

"That's only the start," replied Raven standing up. He pulled up Akio and pulled out his staff. "Run." He said pushing Akio forward who jumped over the hole in the bridge followed by Raven. They ran fast through the halls of the dark fortress. Akio suddenly stopped at a big black door with skull faces for handles.

"Wait. Raven Wait," he said. Raven stopped and hastily went back to Akio. "She's in here. I can feel her." Akio stood back and blasted the door open. The dark creatures rushed the door and Raven and Akio fought their way through. They were almost overwhelmed until Akio got an idea. He took Ravens staff and held it in the air. "Yolanda, close your eyes. Raven you too." Out of the staff Akio produced a brilliant white light that filled the room. The creatures cowered and the un-dead ones started to burn. The others ran from the room leaving only the three of them left. Akio lowered the staff and put out the light.

"Well done Akio. That was fantastic," said Raven who hurried over to Yolanda to untie her. Akio gave the staff back to Raven and readied himself for transportation.

"It won't work in here Akio. There is too much magic against it. We have to get outside the walls of the underworld kingdom. It's why we could never transport in." The last rope was untied and Yolanda jumped into Akio's arms. Raven checked the door. It was clear for now but wouldn't be for long. He gestured for the others to follow him. They couldn't go the way they came, as there were creatures coming for them from that way.

Meanwhile in Danathor, Teju had woken up.

"Teju, I'm afraid you're too late. Yolanda was taken and they have gone to save her," said Garron. Teju got up and put on his cloak.

"Then I shall go after them. Have you anything that flies fast?" he asked. Garron was in shock.

"You're still going in your weakened state?" said Garron. Teju put on his belt and walked over to the door.

"By transporting myself or on the back of a winged steed, I will be going. You can either help me or hinder me." Garron knew there was nothing he could say to change Teju's mind. He had no choice but to help as best he could. He led Teju down to an old barn at the bottom of the kingdom. They opened the door and inside, stood a stone statue of a giant phoenix.

"This is.."

"Vultralite. The phoenix of light," finished Teju, interrupting Garron. "But this legend fell into myth a long time ago. It was said Michael rode him into battle with Raphael. Before he disappeared along with Michael never to be seen again." He turned to Garron.

"This is he," said Garron. "He was found buried near the plains of Belldii. He had turned to stone and it is said that when he is needed to fly again he will revive himself and relight the sky of the dark lands. But your ride is nested behind him." Behind the statue was an adult Chika bird picking at its wing, cleaning itself. "His name is Tweetle. He shall carry you to where you need to go. He is the fastest Chika bird I know. It's why I wanted him." Teju held out his hand and Tweetle hopped up onto his finger. They took him outside where Teju performed the formination spell. Tweetle grew to his large size and Teju climbed on. He shook Garron's hand.

"Thank you Garron."

"See you again my friend," said Garron. Teju and Tweetle then took off and headed north.

Akio, Yolanda and Raven had made their way up into the centre tower trying to head to the main entrance. Raven looked at two different ways to go. He decided to go to the left, which brought them to a long winding staircase.

"I guess we'll have to go up." Said Raven looking up the staircase. They headed up the stairs and as they got higher the air got colder and colder. They came to a huge door and Raven pushed it open. He led them through, but it seemed they had taken a wrong turn. Inside the room waiting was Lord Raphael himself. Chains magically shot from the walls, shackling Akio and Raven to each side of the room. Raphael held out his hand and Yolanda whisked across and into his grasp.

"I've been expecting you, Akio. Do you like my home, or should I say prison?" said Raphael. He sat Yolanda on a chair next to him and chained her to it. He turned his attention back to Akio. "Did you think I would just let you walk in and take the princess, without meeting me? I now know that you are no threat to me until you can wield the sword of Michael." He turned to Raven. "Yes, I know it exists. And I will not give the chance for you in a younger form to strike me down with it. While you two are bound to the walls of my prison palace, I shall send out fleets of evil to rip this world apart." Raven struggled and tried to break free. But the chains were much too tight. Akio tried to use magic to free himself, but his hand was tight to the wall and was unable to move even a little. Raphael laughed as he left the room. Akio and Yolanda struggled to get out of the binds.

"It's no use," said Raven sadly. "We have failed. Once Raphael has destroyed the land he will surely condemn us to the pit of lost souls."

"But why wait to kill me?" Asked Akio. Raven lifted his head and looked at Akio.

"He wants Michael to show himself; it's the only explanation. He wants his revenge. But his pride makes him want to show people he can beat him." He then dropped his head down and became silent.

Days passed and energy faded as they would struggle to get out of their chains. Raven would say nothing and only slightly move at times. Yolanda couldn't keep herself up and was slumped in the chair with only the chains keeping her on it. Akio and Raven, still shackled to the walls, hung there with no fight left. Raphael boldly made his way into the room. He aggressively lifted Raven's head, and dropped it again. He did the same to Akio and then head up to Yolanda.

"Leave her alone," said Akio weakly. Raphael was stunned. He left Yolanda and headed back over to Akio. "If you touch her, I will make you suffer," Akio added. Raphael laughed.

"So there is still fight, the one who means to strike me down." Raphael lifted his arm and walloped Akio's face. Tears came from Yolanda's eyes in seeing this. "Pathetic. Soon enough Michael will show. And when he does, I can finally rid myself of you. And him." Said Raphael who then angrily left the room. Akio dropped his head. There seemed to be no way out of this, and whilst they were held inside the black castle. Raphael's armies were ravishing the outside world. More time passed and the three got more and more anxious. They had no idea what was going on outside these walls. When all hope had seemingly run out, the door slowly opened. It was Teju. He had managed to find his way undetected through the castle.

"Teju. What are you doing here?" Raven said, only barely. Teju hurried to Raven and began to try and break the chains.

"Saving you, my boy." But it seemed Teju had not been as stealthy as he thought. Raphael strode his way back into the room.

"You. I know you. I suppose I owe you some kind of thanks. Had you sent the first Akio after me, I probably wouldn't be so ready for the second." Teju pulled out his wand. And stepped back.

"Raphael," muttered Teju. Raphael laughed. He knew this would be easy.

"You cannot be serious, old man. You wish to fight me? I am Lord Raphael." Teju circled the dark spirit, more frightened than he had ever been. "I have no time for this," said Raphael who shot a single lightning bolt, throwing Teju up in the air and crashing into the ceiling.

"No!" strained Akio and Raven together. Teju came crashing back down and hit the floor hard. But he was already dead. Raven's face was taken by a look of pure anger. He fought to turn his hand in his chains cutting at his wrists. But he couldn't get them to move. He looked at Akio. His eyes were red and there was a faint aura growing strong around his body. It was just like the night back in the forest. Raphael noticed this and threw more chains around Akio. But it would not hold him as he let out an unbelievable rush of power, breaking his chains and knocking Raphael backwards. He broke Raven's chains and turned to check Raphael. He was up and bowled his way over to Akio. He smacked Akio across the room and shot a bolt of lightning, but Akio was quick enough to avoid it. When Raven had freed Yolanda he stumbled over to the door. Akio rolled over and they all ran as fast as they could towards the main door. They ran down the stairs and down the corridor. They came to another door, but it was locked. Akio blasted it open and they ran down the ramp. They ran past different creatures that started to chase after them. They were all still tired from being held captive. They ran outside and made their way to the gate. But they would have to fly over, and neither Akio nor Raven knew if they had the strength. But then, the large Chika bird that had brought Teju swooped down and picked them up. They had narrowly escaped the black castle, but at the cost of Teju's life. The journey back would be filled with heartache and pain.

After a couple of days they stopped by a stream to eat and clean themselves up. When Tweetle landed, Raven jumped straight off and kicked a tree branch hard. He screamed out in anger and shot a fireball at a tree. Akio had walked into the stream and looked at the horizon, a tear streaming down his face. Yolanda walked up to Raven and handed him an apple pulled from a nearby apple tree. She then went up to Akio and held his hand. She led him out of the stream and they all sat together with Yolanda sitting in the middle.

"He should never have come for us," said Raven. Yolanda placed her hand on Raven and said.

"Maybe so. But if he hadn't the war would have already been over. The skies would have turned black and death would have been inevitable." Raven knew that she was right. It was just hard to see a man who had been like a father for such a long time killed right before his eyes, with him helpless at the side lines. They slept for the night by the stream. Akio was restless. He had to finish this, fulfil the prophecy.

In the morning they got back onto Tweetle's back and headed for Hera. But when they got there, no one was around. The city was in ruin and there were bodies left from a battle that had happened days before. They were too late. Akio and Raven were speechless. They couldn't help but feel at fault. Their absence had affected things in just a matter of days. But Yolanda remembered something.

"My father always said that when things got out of hand, men would head to the underground City of Mothe. They might be there. In fact I'm sure they are there." Raven had never seen this part of the world.

"You can direct us there?" he asked Yolanda. She nodded insistently.

"Yes, my dad would recite the rhyme to me every night when I was young. He said it was our secret. The monks of Gresh and the Narrca Sea, you will see the boulder, so clearly. Land in front, and give it a shunt, and you will find our underground city."

"Then that's where we shall go," stated Raven jumping back onto Tweetle's back. The other two joined him and Tweetle took to the sky. They past the mountain path of Gresh and flew on. They passed by the Narrca Sea, and Akio looked down. The sea was beautiful and clear. He saw a whale come to the surface and blow water high out of its blowhole. Yolanda then saw it.

"Down there," said Yolanda pointing to a boulder in the ground. Tweetle headed down and landed just next to the bolder. Raven took his staff from his back and hopped off Tweetle's back. He walked up to the bolder and moved it aside. Stairs were revealed and Raven turned Tweetle back to normal size and the three headed down.

"Why are all the hidden places underground?" asked Akio.

"The natural heat of the earth makes for a perfect hideaway. If need be, plants and crops can be grown and it will never get cold. It is also more secure than a wall that can be knocked down," he replied. "They were built by the Dwarves before they all died out."

"Died out? There are no more Dwarves at all?" Akio asked, surprised as they continued down the stairway passage.

"Not for a long while now. No one knows where they went, or even if or how they died. But they left all there underground cities, as if they had planned to return one day. But they just never did."

A door appeared and Raven knocked three times. There was one knock back. Yolanda said,

"Now knock twice." So Raven did and the door then opened. Inside the mass underground city, beings from all over the land had come. There were Elves and the Elvor, Centurions and Fawns, men from Hera, Danathor, the east and the west. Yolanda saw her father and caught his eye. Garron dropped his goblet and smiled a huge smile.

"Yolanda," he muttered to himself running over to her. They embraced strongly, but Garron noticed that they were one short.

"Where is Teju?" he asked. Raven and Akio looked at each other and Raven just shook his head.

"He didn't make it?" Garron then called for attention across the vast underground city.

"My friends and fellow warriors." The crowds died down and turned to pay attention. "A star will shine whether the sky wishes it or not. A tree still grows after being embedded with an axe. And a man still believes when all others turn their faith. Today we mourn the death of that man. A man who without question held more care for this world than we who lived blind. It was he who prophesized the coming of the war, and it is true to say, that had it not been for him, we would not breathe even this musky underground air we fill our lungs with now. A better man than me dies for a cause that affects us all. And we will honour him. To Teju." The crowd cheered and raised their arms to Teju's memory.

After his speech Garron went up to Raven and Akio.

"Garron. Raphael knows about the sword of Michael. I trust you did not leave it in Danathor?" Garron's face already revealed the truth.

"I had no choice my friend. It does not let anyone touch it. It can only be held by the one it's supposed to." Raven thought for a moment. And then turned back to Garron.

"Raphael spoke of Michael returning, but the prophecy states that a boy named Akio would strike down the Dark Lord of the underworld and bring peace. But it does not allow him either. Which are we to believe?" Both were confused. They knew however that it would mean that Raphael could never wield the sword. At least they were safe from that. They would have to figure it out on their own, as Teju was no longer around to answer the questions of the prophecy.

Over the next couple of hours, Raven, Mr. Yama, Garron, Mrs. Fritter and Bogal went over all they knew about the prophecy and the war. Raven at last had to explain to those who didn't know who he really was. But it seemed Teju had already filled them in. The first time this had happened, Teju had hidden Raven from Raphael and thus no war took place. They also knew that time would not allow this, so had sent Akio back to finish what had started. Akio could not yet touch the sword of Michael, but neither could Raven. They talked about how Yolanda must be kept as safe and as hidden as possible due to the feelings she and Akio felt for each other. Raphael had already tried to use that for himself. The vital point of what they knew was that it would have to be Akio who landed the final blow to Raphael. But with the possible return of Michael, they didn't know if it would be with the sword in the prophecy.

Akio had decided that as much as it hurt, he must try to suppress his feeling for Yolanda. She came over and took his hand. He pulled away and walked over to a ledge looking into the city. Confused, Yolanda tried again. But again Akio shunned her off. Had his feelings changed? she thought.

Over in the meeting, a plan had still not been made. Things had changed too much since the quest had first been decided.

"We cannot fight." Said Bogal. "Their forces are too many, to the point in which beings from all over have been driven to an underground refuge. We have lost the man who knew anything about this war and we have a hero who cannot wield his own weapon that will strike down the enemy. No plan we could devise can see us through this mess." Garron banged on the table.

"So you suggest we cower here forever?" he asked.

"Why not wait for Michael if he is to return?" asked Bogal. "He banished him once before. This time he can finish him off." Raven stood and placed his hands on the table.

"Because not only do we not know if he will return. That is not what is written." Bogal was growing tired of the prophecy.

"We have to stop thinking of this as some kind of foretold story. The prophecy said Akio would wield the sword. He can't. The prophecy is a lie. And we have to take to this with tactics and attack methods." Akio heard the five arguing and decided it was time he said something for himself. He walked up to the table and called for hush.

"Teju believed in the prophecy. He believed so much he was willing to give his life to save mine. I don't know why I can't wield the sword yet. But if he thought the time would come. Then it will, and I shall strike Raphael down. I am ready to do what I must, I've waited long enough." The show of confidence seemed to soothe the others. It had gotten late and it was time to eat. They would leave it for now, as they would be safe underground. With the knowledge that Raphael was waiting for the return of Michael to kill Akio meant that they were in better stead than they had been before, even if it didn't seem so.

Early the next morning, Akio was learning to smoke a pipe with some men from Hera. Raven came up and tapped him on the shoulder.

"Akio, we have decided that myself, you and Bogal are going to return to Danathor and see if there is anything we missed. We should be able to transport. Raphael should leave you be for now if he really is waiting for Michael." Akio got up and said goodbye to the men of Hera. They went over to where Mr. Yama, Bogal and Garron were waiting. Bogal stepped forward and then the three of them head for the exit. Yolanda saw them leaving and ran over to try and say goodbye to Akio. But he didn't even turn his head. Upset, she went back to reading her book. It hurt him to do it, but any feelings he had for Yolanda would put her in danger. He had to try and confuse Raphael's sight.

The Three then transported to Danathor. It had been completely destroyed. The only still standing walls were the ones that housed the sword of Michael.

"Reduced to a wasteland," Akio whispered to himself. Raven and Bogal went up to the room and went inside. It was like it hadn't been touched. It was strange. Proudly still displayed were the sword and shield. Akio wandered in and Raven motioned for him to try and take it. Akio stepped up and held out his hand. He got closer, but when he got too close, again the sword and shield denied him. No one knew what it would take for the sword to surrender to Akio.

"Bogal. You can read the scriptures on the wall. Have we missed anything?" asked Raven. Bogal went over to the start of the wall and started to read through. He moved along the wall reading and looking at the paintings.

"It just keeps referring to 'The One'. Nothing seems to be missing." said Bogal. What was the answer? Raven picked up Akio. They could do no more good here. They went back outside and prepared to transport.

In the underworld castle Raphael was pacing up and down. A rogue ran in.

"My lord. It's here." Raphael stopped pacing and pushed past. He hurried outside to see the statue of Vultralite being carried in. Raphael was sure that when Michael returned, he would seek out his old steed. Which would mean he would have to come to the underworld. Then he would strike.

"Set it down right there in the middle," he shouted to those carrying it. He believed that now, he had an edge.

Disappointed, Raven, Akio and Bogal went back to the underground city of Mothe. But they did not have any answers. They were at a loss at what to do next. Every second Raphael waited. He produced more for his armies.

Yolanda came up to Akio.

"How did it go?" she asked Akio, who sat down and took off his gauntlets.

"Not good," he said, annoyed. He slammed down his gauntlets and kicked off his boots. "How can I do what is needed if the source won't accept me. How can I fulfil the prophecy?" He got up and picked up his boots and gauntlets and threw them in a corner. He took off his sword and went over to a bed. He lay down and turned his back. Again disappointed, Yolanda decided to leave him be.

That night, when all were asleep, Akio lay awake. So many things were going through his mind. The entire world was counting on him to end this war. But the only thing that would make him able to do that was denying him from even touching it. He wondered if Michael would return and what it would mean for the prophecy. The more he thought, the more he had the idea that all hope was lost. A small ball of light then floated into the city. It came over to Akio and hovered over his face. Akio sat up and tried to touch it. The ball of light flew around his head frantically and then moved away from him. Akio decided to follow it. It led him down the big grand staircase and across the centre. Down and down they went further underground, until they came to a small alcove with a wooden ladder leading upwards. The ball of light shot up until out of sight. Akio stepped onto the ladder and started to climb. It went on for a while and Akio wondered if it would ever stop. He then came to small wooden door, so he crouched down and went through. On the other side he came out halfway up a gargantuan tree. There were lanterns scattered about hanging on the branches. All around him were different-coloured little lights, millions of them. One came in really close and Akio realised that they were fairies. He held out his hand and it landed in his palm. It did a little curtsy and then flew off again. Another flew over. This one was a male. He did a little bow and then flew off. After that hundreds of them flew over and took hold of Akio. They lifted him up and flew up the tree. They placed him down on the top of the tree, when a bigger fairy came out of the sky. It circled Akio and then landed in front of him. It bowed and began to speak.

"Akio. Imagination is the key. To find the one you wish to seek. Flash of light, at the break of night. And the two of you shall finally meet." The fairy then flew off and joined the others. Two of the smaller fairies then flew over and went in Akio's pocket and pulled out the map. They opened it up and started to prance around on it. The whole thing lit up and slowly appearing in a blank spot, a new place was being revealed. They then flew away leaving Akio with the map. They must have wanted him to go there, but what for?

Akio stood up and bowed to the fairies that picked him up again and flew him back down to the little door. Akio went back through and went back down the ladder. He returned to the city and went back to his bed. In the morning he would show Raven.

Morning came and Akio went over to where Raven was sleeping.

"Raven. Raven, wake up," said Akio shaking him. Raven turned over and looked at Akio. He sat up and rubbed his eyes.

"What is it, Akio?" Akio pulled out the map and opened it up.

"Last night I was taken to the fairy tree. They revealed this place on the map for me. They must want us to go there." Raven looked stunned and took hold of the map for a look.

"The fairy tree? I know of no such place." He saw the new place on the map. "I do not know of this place either," he said. Raven put his hand to his chin. What was this fairy tree, he hadn't been taken there the first time although the time line had already changed. They would have to find this place and find out what it was. He looked up at Akio.

"Suit up." The two got ready and Garron came over.

"Are you sure about this Raven? The fairies haven't shown themselves since the disappearance of Michael, how do we know they can be trusted?" Raven sighed and looked up.

"I don't, but at the moment. It's all we have." Raven and Akio then head out of the city. When outside Akio took out the map and looked at the place they were going.

"Can we transport to it? We wouldn't have known it existed if it hadn't been found for us," said Akio worried they would have to walk. Raven thought for a moment, they could try. They closed their eyes and transported. Whilst in transportation they seemed to be caught in some kind of vortex. It threw them around like a hurricane, until it violently threw them out and on to the ground. They picked themselves up and looked around. They had landed in a baron dessert land with nothing but a big golden temple in front of them. They brushed themselves off and went up to the entranceway. Cautiously they made their way inside. Inside was completely hollowed out and in the middle stood a giant gold statue of a man holding a sword high in the air. Raven noticed that the sword he was holding was the sword of Michael.

"It's a monument to Michael." Raven ran around trying to find clues. He knocked on the stone plinth it stood on and on the last side it opened up and a scroll fell out. He picked up the scroll and started reading. It was a log of the battle from years past. While Raven was reading Akio stood in awe of the statue. He then remembered what the fairy had said.

"Raven, it has to be just as the sun goes down." Raven stopped reading.

"Really? How do you know this?" Akio took the scroll and placed it on the ground.

"The fairy said. Imagination is the key. To find the one you wish to seek. Flash of light, at the break of night. And the two of you shall finally meet. I assume at the last light, the door will reveal itself." Raven nodded and they both sat waiting for the sun to go down.

When it finally did, Akio stepped forward to the statue. He didn't know what to do so thought he would just speak from the heart.

"I stand before you a man at loss. Look at me. I am just a boy from a normal world, not even ready for a weapon I'm supposed to wield. The prophecy of a world I didn't even know existed. I will end this war for you. But I need your help." Nothing happened. But then he remembered back. All the way back to what the bus driver had said to him. He had said to never let his mind become clear. The map worked on Akio's mind, so maybe this would too. Akio closed his eyes and imagined Michael's statue glowing. Raven stood up astonished, for the real statue was glowing too. Then a bright flash filled the sky destroying the roof of the temple and a beam of light shot down and lit up the room. Michael himself walked from the blinding light. He had returned.

Michael was tall and broad. He stopped in front of his statue and the light faded away. He looked around and then saw Akio standing a bit away.

"Young Akio, I knew you would come." Raven and Akio were both speechless. This was the one that had banished Raphael and brought peace. "I can imagine there are a lot of unanswered questions and I will answer them all. After setting me free, I owe you that Akio." He stretched himself out and cracked his neck. Akio got himself together and started to ask his questions.

"Where have you been all this time?" asked Akio.

"Raphael is my brother and in banishment of him our connection seemed severed. But I was foolish. I bound Raphael's banishment to myself to keep him from returning. But it was not strong enough. When he came back, my power faded and I was left in the non-world." He turned to Akio and placed his hand on his shoulder. "Until a boy would come, and free me from myself. And here you are Akio." Raven stepped up. There were some things he wanted to know too.

"Your sword. Why is it that they were left? Why didn't they go with you? Can't you wield them to end this war?"

"I'm afraid I left them for a purpose. Had you not figured out how to free me, someone would have to destroy Raphael. So I left them for someone else, the boy of destiny. And that is why I cannot wield them. They are not mine anymore." Time was wasting and they knew they would have to get back.

In the underworld castle Raphael had felt the massive surge of energy.

"Can it be?" he said to himself. The feeling was very familiar. His brother must have returned. This was it; he couldn't miss his chance. He must lure his brother here using Vultralite. He got up and went outside as fast as he could. "Get out of the way." He said pushing rogues aside. He went up to Vultralite and examined it. How could he summon Michael to it? There were no markings or scripture of any kind. Frustrated he kicked the statue and threw a lightning bolt, killing a nearby goblin. "How does this work!" he cried.

Akio, Raven and Michael had returned to the underground city of Mothe. As they entered everyone stopped to look. Muttering filled the city as Michael stepped in.

"I don't believe it," said Garron astonished. "Michael has returned." Mr. Yama and Mrs. Fritter joined them, jaws dropped. Mr Yama touched Michael.

"Can it be true? Are you really here?" Michael took Mr Yama's hand and shook it.

"Yes my friend. But please," he exclaimed to everyone. "Times have changed. My brother is a lot stronger. But I can assure you, I will do all I can to bring an end to dark times." He went over to Akio. "And as long as this man lives. Hope still remains." The crowd cheered. Akio pulled Michael to one side.

"Can't you just change it? You made this world. Can't you just put things right?" Michael sat Akio down.

"You have to understand Akio. I've been away a long, long time. This is not the same world. I poured my life force into creating a world; when Raphael betrayed me, I used what little was left on banishing him. I used the last I had on leaving my sword and shield for the one that would bring peace. In this world Akio, you have more power than me." Akio didn't know what to say. It seemed all for nothing. They were no better off freeing Michael than they were before. Nothing made sense anymore. He flopped down sitting next to Michael.

"So there is no hope?"

"Hope can always be found, Akio. Sometimes there seems to be no way forward. And in those times, there seems to be no way back either. I can do a number of things. But one thing I can't is destroy my brother. But you, Akio are the way forward." He stood up and looked over at Raven talking with the others. "I didn't expect to see two of you. So it's even different from the way it was supposed to be." Akio joined him.

"Teju taught Raven all he knew the first time." Michael then remembered Teju.

"Yes, Teju. I managed to communicate to him the prophecy. Where is he?" asked Michael wanting to meet the man he had spoken to all those years ago. Akio dropped his head in disappointment.

"I'm afraid he is no longer with us. Raphael struck him down. He did it to save my life." Michael looked shocked and appalled. The look then changed to a look of sadness.

"I'm sorry, Akio. I never meant for any of this to happen. I'm sorry I got you into all of this." They stood together looking over the city. Somehow they had to fix all of this.

"Why is it the sword still won't let me near?" asked Akio.

"I don't know I'm afraid Akio. There's something wrong, something it won't accept." Akio sensed an irritation on Michael's part. Deep down he must have known that at some point he would have to face his brother. Akio left him to his thoughts and went down to see the others. On his way Yolanda confronted him.

"Akio. I have been trying to understand why your feelings you expressed are fading. Maybe your more a mystery than I thought. But…Just be careful." She then quickly made her way away from him in tears. Akio was only doing what he thought was for the best, but it hurt him so much. He began to anger. Everything was falling apart so quickly. With that he stormed his way outside and climbed onto a high rock.

"I have had enough! Raphael! I, Akio am calling out to you for us to end this war!" he cried out in anger.

In the underworld castle, Raphael heard the cry. Maybe it was time for the final war of this world.

"Vigo!" shouted Raphael. Vigo came running in. "It's time. Gather every being you can find with the will of evil. We shall answer his call. This world will be mine!" Vigo nodded and ran out of the room. Raphael sat seething. His plan had not worked. But he knew that Michael would be with them, so he would still get his chance.

Chapter 7

The Last War

Raphael strolled out the entrance of his black castle. Thousands of creatures awaited orders. Vigo was running around, conjuring more un-dead from the ground below and placing them in the ranks.

Michael felt this. He ran down to Garron, Akio, Bogal and Raven who were sitting together reading scrolls they had found.

"It's happening. It seems he has answered your call Akio," said Michael hastily. The others shot up and ran into the main centre of the city.

"Get everyone you can. Arm them and get them outside. We march north," said Garron. Akio and Raven went to suit up. They grabbed their swords, knives and put on their armour. Raven picked up his staff and went up to Akio.

"This is it, Akio. I can't tell you what will happen. But now we must give all that we are. Every bit of power and every bit of will, this, is it. You have to let it all go. I know you can do it." Akio nodded, his heart beating faster than it ever had before. Ultimately, this all came down to him. Back out in the city, men, elves elvor, monks and all such manner of beings assembled and started to make their way out of the city. Raven and Akio joined Bogal and Garron outside, watching as they all ascended from the underground. Yolanda ran out and before he could notice jumped on Akio giving him a huge hug. She was in tears and hysterics.

"This may be the last time I see you. I'm not sure what has come between us in the days past, but I couldn't let you leave without telling you." She looked in his eyes. They both felt a connection that filled their hearts and there was a glint in their eyes. "I love you Akio. You make me feel like hope isn't just a feeling, but a complete possibility. Come back to me. Please?" Akio welled up. He could not continue the charade any longer. He placed his hands softly on her face and kissed her quivering lips.

"I love you too, Yolanda. I'm sorry. I felt I needed to protect you. If there has been anything I have been sure about since being in this world, it's how I felt about you when I first saw you. If there is any strength in me, it has come from you." He touched his hand to her chin. "I will come back to you." Michael joined them and Yolanda went back into the City.

"The strongest a man can be, is through how much he loves. Remember that Akio," said Michael commenting on what he had just seen. "You will feel that strength on the battle field."

They all then watched as thousands of troops formed up outside.

"An army of light for a war that will go down in history," exclaimed Garron. When all had lined up Garron, Akio, Raven, Bogal and Michael took the helm. Michael then signalled for the move forward, and the army of light marched for the gates of the underworld. Everything had come down to this, the final war. Each army from both sides marched through the night, only stopping for minutes at a time. Vigo led the army of darkness, while Raphael remained in his castle. He knew Akio did not have the sword. But if they would have their final confrontation, it would be on his ground. Akio would have to come to him.

"What about the sword?" Akio asked Michael. But Michael didn't know.

"Maybe I was wrong, Akio. I don't know. It's hard to see anything I'm afraid." It seemed the only answers Akio would find would be in the battle they marched towards. The land seemed empty. As if every being in this world had chosen a side. And all that existed was the two armies marching towards their fate.

The army arrived on the field of Roul, the last field before the sky grew dark. In the distance the army of darkness waited, with Vigo at the front. The two armies stood for a moment, as everything grew silent. The final war was seconds away and the tension grew to new heights. Fear filled the ranks to the point where even grown men were losing the control of their bodily functions. Beings trembled and some started to cry. There seemed no better time for the heavens to open and the rain begin to fall. Time seemed to be trickling by so slowly. It was literally like waiting for death. Vigo lifted his mace. He held it there for a moment, and then when he dropped it down the dark army began to advance. Garron motioned for the army of light to move forward. Neither army ran to start with and the rain picked up. Akio's heart was still beating hard. He then remembered all the way back to when he had arrived in this world. Mr. Yama's voice filled his head saying.

"Akio my boy, just remember. What saves a man is to take a step, then another step. It is always the same step, but it gets you to where you are. You took that first step on to that bus, and it led you here, now all you have to do, is keep on stepping, and you'll find yourself to be somewhere else. Life is a journey Akio, and we are the ones who choose where to step next."

Akio then swallowed hard and then charged the dark army, which began to run themselves. Garron motioned for them to do the same. The forces collided, the army of light severely outnumbered. But with Akio, Raven and Michael, they were holding on. Carnage to the left, carnage to the right and as far as the eye could see. It was a sea of destruction. The ground was trampled in seconds leaving only a pit of mud and slush. Explosions, streams of blood and cries from the dying and wounded filled the air. Akio fought his way through the masses using a combination of magic and his trusty sword. Lightning struck and Akio came face to face with Vigo. He ran swinging his mace closer to Akio, who jumped out of the way. He ran again bringing his mace over his head. Akio quickly raised his sword and blocked the incoming weapon. But it was heavy and it knocked him to his knees. Vigo reset and went to swing at Akio's head. Noticing this, Akio flew up into the air and came down striking with his sword. He missed but turned and cast a spell that knocked Vigo back, but he remained standing. Michael looked over and shouted to Akio.

"Don't be afraid anymore. You have the power Akio. Let it free!" Akio looked deep inside and felt the fire within. He thought about home, Yolanda, Tiny and Teju. The more he thought the more the fire grew. The thought of what would happen if he failed. The look in Akio's eyes then changed. Once again it was the look he had that night in the forest with Raven. He strode up to Vigo, who seeing the look in Akio's eyes, cowered away. He swung his mace, but Akio burst out an aura knocking it from his hands. Vigo scrambled backwards but Akio followed. He held his sword up and backed Vigo to a tree. He held his blade to Vigo's throat.

"I suppose you're going to kill me now," said Vigo tensing up. Akio leant in with his blade held in position.

"No. You go and tell your master, that I am coming. I'm releasing you from this battlefield." He then lowered his sword and let Vigo go. Vigo ran past him and Akio didn't even turn his head. Vigo ran, until he got closer to where Michael was standing. From under his rags Vigo pulled out a small glowing black blade. As Akio turned around, Vigo ran up to a distracted Michael and stabbed him in the back with the blade. Michael yelled out in pain as a black mist came out of his wound. Akio shouted and ran up to Michael catching him in his arms. The battle raged on around them and Vigo had made himself scarce.

"What was that, what's happening?" asked Akio frantically. Michael gasped for breath as more black mist came from where the blade had stabbed him.

"It was the Vesteele, a dagger made by our father. Raphael must have given it to him. My life force is draining. Even now he is too cowardly to face me himself." Akio felt useless holding him there in his arms.

As they knelt in the middle of the battlefield, over in the courtyard of the underworld, Vultralite began to awaken. The stone that was once a statue gradually transformed back into the phoenix itself. Raphael ran to the window on hearing the great birdcall. When the transformation was complete, Vultralite started to flap its big wings and flew off away from the castle. Raphael shouted out in annoyance. If the bird got to Michael, it could save his life. His cowardliness at not taking on Michael himself may have cost him the chance of killing his brother.

Vultralite flew faster than anything had before getting to Michael and Akio in minutes. Just before he scooped him up, Michael pulled off his necklace, and hanging on the chain was a crystal.

"Put this on Akio, It's all I can give. I'm sorry I failed you Akio." Michael and Vultralite then took off and flew out of sight. Akio stood clutching the crystal in his hand. The environment around him came back into focus and Akio drew his sword once more and returned to the fight. A new fire and passion shone through Akio, striking down all that came near him. It was a will of anger and hate. His speed increased, his strike strengthened and he began to produce a dark red aura around him. Raven looked on, worried that Akio was close to the edge. If his heart did not remain pure, he may never be able to finish Raphael. Raven flew over to Akio and landed behind him. Without a thought, Akio turned and kicked Raven back and leapt up into the air, landing with his sword drawn to Raven. Raven lay back putting his hands up.

"It's me Akio, It's me. Try to find the light. What would Yolanda think?" In saying that Akio's mind went into a fritz. The crystal in his hand started to glow. He realized what he was doing. He pulled his sword away and stumbled backward before falling to his knees. There it was, exactly as Mrs. Fritters book had showed it. The sky was black, the land was destroyed and bodies lay all around. It had all come true. He realized then that he needed to consult that book. Raven got up and went over to Akio, who looked up at him.

"You need to go don't you Akio," he said. Akio stood up and nodded.

"This is just like it showed it, I can't believe this is all coming true." Raven pulled him up. "Go, we'll hold things here." Akio and Raven hugged, then Akio transported himself to Skye City.

Once there, Akio ran through the deserted streets to Mrs. Fritters inn. In a frantic hurry Akio kicked down the door and rushed into the sitting room. The book was sitting on a corner table and Akio ran over to it trying to remember what it was Mr. Yama had done. He thought back and then remembered. Akio took out his wand and picked up an envelope that was lying next to where the book had been. He tapped the page with his wand. He didn't know any of the spells so just thought of what he wanted to know. He pulled a stream of light from the page and put it in the envelope. He threw the envelope onto the logs in the fireplace and conjured a fireball and lit the logs. The fire burst out blue and then died down. A picture began to appear. It showed the underworld with Akio and Raven standing in an auditorium like room. Raven faded from the sight, leaving just Akio and Raphael one to one on top of the tallest tower of the underworld kingdom with Akio holding the sword of Michael. The picture then fell back into the fire and the fire went out. Still confused, Akio decided to try again. He got another envelope and tapped another page. Again he threw it into the fire and lit the logs. This time the picture was harder to see. It was blurred and Akio could barely make out what was going on. He squinted his eyes but it didn't really help. The picture then turned back into a stream of light and jumped over into the book. It read:

"When times change it is hard to see. What the future holds for thee. Where to look, may be not in a book, but in the heart of me." Akio tried to look in his heart but did not find any answers. It must be referring to Raven. For Raven was Akio.

That was enough for now as time was short. Akio closed the book and left it on the chair running back out of the inn. He thought while he was here he would quickly visit Tiny's grave, so made his way over. He knelt down and put a seed down on the grave, before transporting back to the battlefield. When he arrived not much had changed, hundreds still remained.

"What did you find?" shouted Raven running over. Akio blocked an oncoming attack before turning to Raven and saying,

"We have to get this to the underworld. The war ends there." Raven knew there would only be one way of getting them all to the underworld, but even so they weren't all connected so it wouldn't work.

"How do we do that Akio? We can't transport them, we would all have to be touching." Akio thought for a moment. Raven was right, there were still hundreds left and unless they were all connected it wouldn't be possible. He was then struck with an idea. He pulled out the crystal that Michael had given him and held it in the air. He began to glow so brightly that it caught everyone's attention. Raven figured out what Akio was doing and shouted for all the light army to run towards Akio. The army of the underworld was intrigued by this object and was lured towards it. Everyone crashed together and in that moment Raven and Akio performed the transportation. They landed in the underworld, but as expected Raven and Akio had weakened themselves. Garron came over and picked up Raven, he shouted to Bogal to aid Akio. They dragged them away from harm and returned to the battle. The crystal around Akio's neck started to float and glow. Akio felt his strength return. He sat up and held it over Raven. He too regained some strength.

Raphael hurried over to his window. The fight had been brought to him. For the first time he felt a real sense of fear, but he noticed that Akio did not have the sword. He smiled and then jumped out of the window and flew down to the ground. He landed with a thunderous thud right in front of Akio and Raven. Raphael pulled out a big battered sword and held it out in front of him, Akio and Raven then drew theirs. Raphael swung and the duel commenced.

The three of them fought their way through the battle and into the castle. They brawled through the entrance hall and over to a staircase. Vigo came running in from the door and intervened. Akio blocked the shot and the two of them split off. Still angry at what Vigo had done, Akio over powered him. He hit hard and knocked Vigo to the ground. He kicked his weapon across the room and Vigo cowered on the floor.

"Mercy," Vigo spluttered. Akio stopped in disbelief of what Vigo had said.

"Mercy? Mercy? Did you show mercy? Has Raphael showed mercy? You know, all this time I didn't think I had the strength to get through this. Before I came here I had never even held a sword let alone taken a life." He raised his sword up. "And now I know what I have to do." Vigo slowly stood up as Akio started to swing his sword, and with one fell swing he cut through Vigo's neck, cutting off his head. Vigo's body fell to the ground and Akio turned around to see that Raven and Raphael had gone. He left the body and ran to find them.

Outside, high on a connecting bridge Raven and Raphael were still battling with each other. Raphael kicked Raven back and let out a big laugh.

"Haven't you figured it out yet?" Raven looked confused. "Have you not thought why Akio couldn't use the sword? It came to me when thinking about the prophecy. It refers to one. Not two." Everything started to make sense and it all fell into place. "We can fight for as long as you want, but as long as I keep you alive, he can never wield the sword of Michael. You can never win." Raven couldn't believe he had missed it.

"That's why you didn't kill us when you had us captive. It wasn't Akio you were keeping alive. It was me.

That's why you never attacked the first time. You wanted time to repeat itself, because while there were two of us, you couldn't be defeated. As long as there were two of us, we would always lose. All of this has all been a front. You knew from the start." Raphael stood smirking at Raven. Akio got up to where they were and appeared at the archway. Raven turned his head to Akio, then back at Raphael. There was only one way for Akio to use the sword and one way to win the war. He looked down at the battle still going on in the underworld courtyard. Garron and Bogal both looked up high to see them all on the bridge. Raven sheathed his sword and put his staff on his back. He turned to face the edge. For there to be one, Raven would have to die. He then leapt into the air off the bridge and free fell all the way down. Akio ran forward and trying to grab hold, but he missed. Before he knew it Raven had hit the ground. Tears streamed from Akio's eyes and he stood up angrier than he had ever been. Realizing the situation Raphael summoned a black dragon and quickly jumped on its back. Akio screamed out in anger and flew up into the air, but he could not keep up with them. But from up high a flash of orange light pierced through the clouds and Vultralite swooped down. He flew under Akio and caught him on his back. They then flew fast catching up with Raphael.

"Wait," said Akio realizing what this meant. "Vultralite, we need to go to Danathor. Get ready." Akio then closed his eyes and transported them both back to Danathor. Vultralite landed and Akio jumped off and headed to the room with the sword. He walked in and held out his hand. This time the sword started to shake and leapt of it plinth and into Akio's hand. Holding it felt like electricity, more power than ever. Akio ran out to Vultralite and transported back. He looked around for Raphael. He saw him in the distance and Vultralite flew fast towards him. The two clashed in the air Michaels sword destroying Raphael's blade. He flew away but Akio followed. They got side by side and Akio swung at the dragon. He sliced through its neck and Raphael and the dragon plummeted down to the tower top. Akio and Vultralite landed and Akio got off. He walked over to Raphael, clutching the sword strongly. Raphael noticed Akio.

"So this is it is it? You're going to save the world? You're nothing, Akio." Akio continued forward.

"Really? Maybe I was, but not now. I'm going to finish this." As Akio went to strike, Raphael kicked the sword form his hand. He jumped up and the two both threw spells at the same time and they both went flying backwards. They got up and ran at each other, but with Raphael being bigger and stronger Akio was at the disadvantage. Raphael hit him in the face, blood spurting from Akio's mouth. He struck Akio again, knocking him down to his hands and knees. A kick to the stomach sent him up and a kick back sent Akio hurtling towards the edge of the tower top. Akio noticed how close he got and spun round to stop himself. He picked himself up and looked for the sword. It was over by the other edge teetering over. He ran for it, but Raphael intercepted him lifting him up and slamming him to the floor. The floor broke beneath him almost falling through. Akio once again tried to pick himself up, but was taken hold of by Raphael. He put his big hand around Akio's neck and started to squeeze.

"Did you honestly think it would be that easy? Just get the sword and everything would be fine? I am the lord of the underworld, not some mere peasant like you. My power may have decreased over time, but I am still more than you can ever hope to be. Who are you?" Akio struggled and choked, pulling on Raphael's arm. But with the last breath it seemed he had he forced out the words.

"I am Akio." A rush of energy erupted from Akio's body, breaking Raphael's grip. Akio dropped down only just landing on his feet. He threw himself over towards the sword that was slowly slipping off the edge. He got it just in time.

"No!" Shouted Raphael lunging for Akio. Akio caught the sword and turned on his back holding it out. The sword pierced Raphael, breaking through amour, clothing and flesh, and a black blood trickled out of the wound. Raphael stumbled backwards pulling himself off the sword and placing his hands to the slice. His body started to turn to ash and from his centre he then exploded. As the explosion happened everything began to quake. All the evil creatures tried to run away but were turning into ash themselves. Raphael's explosion was so strong the underworld began to crumble.

"Run, save yourselves!" shouted Garron to the soldiers left on the battlefield. He looked up, as Akio was still on top of the tower. The castle began to collapse and debris rained from the sky. Garron had no choice but to get clear. A huge hole emanated from under the castle and the underworld was pulled inside. The tower crashed down destroying the rest of the castle. When everyone was clear, sand and dirt filled the air, so thick it was hard to see through it. All that was left was a cliff edge with the rubble that had been the underworld in a piled mess down below. When the dust settled, Garron hurried over to the ledge and peered over.

"Akio!" he shouted. "Akio!"

Akio had not gotten out in time. He dropped to a knee and put his arm to his chest as a sign of respect for the fallen hero. The war was over.

Bogal came over and joined him.

"He didn't get out did he?" Garron said nothing and just shook his head. Bogal went to the edge and stuck his sword in the ground. The two then turned and joined the others. They had little more than a quarter of the ones they had started with. The ones that remained then started their long walk back to the underground city.

The walk was long and tiring for those who were left, but they trudged on with the strength they had left. But after a long time walking, the city entrance was in sight. Garron could see Yolanda awaiting their return. She saw them coming and saw her father, but Akio was nowhere in sight. Her heart fell and eyes welled up. When Garron reached where she was standing she looked at him so anxiously.

"Where is he?" she asked. Garron dropped his head as a tear fell from his eye. She knew what it meant and fell to the ground, crying.

"I'm sorry my dear. There was nothing anyone could do. The castle fell and he had tired from the battle with Raphael." But Garron knew that no words could console her. Her heart felt like it had shattered into a million pieces. Garron helped her to her feet and gave her a big hug. "He saved us Yolanda. He did it." They went inside and Yolanda ran off in tears. Garron himself had still not gotten over what he had seen and all that had transpired. To save everyone else, a young boy had come, and given his life for a cause he didn't quite understand. In the short time Akio had been there, he had made an impression on them all. Not just as the chosen one, but as a friend.

Races returned to their parts of the world and tried to rebuild what they could. Time past and grass re-grew, kingdoms were re-built and the sky had never been clearer. Peace had finally come to the dream world and in the centre of Danathor a statue was erected of the fallen hero Akio. Things seemed to return to normal. But for Yolanda, things had never been so different. She would walk the gardens of Danathor, like she used to, but her spirit was not the same. She was sitting on a bench near a beautiful white blossom tree, when Garron came over and joined her.

"I can see you are still hurting my dear. I wish there was something I could do." She buried herself into her father's arms and hugged him tightly. Garron looked up at the tree and thought of something to say.

"You know. My mother, your grandmother, planted this tree years ago. She never saw it bloom, as she died before it was fully grown. But she did not plant it for her. She planted it here so that future generations would have a chance to see its beauty." He lifted her chin. "Akio gave his life, so that you, others and future generations could live a full and better life. Just as she would have liked to see this tree bloom, we all wanted to see Akio return with us. But we have to focus on what his sacrifice gave to us. He gave us the chance to see a new beauty." Yolanda wiped her eyes and looked up at the blossom tree.

"We should say goodbye properly." she said. Garron smiled.

"Now that's a good idea. We shall gather the people in the city square and have a proper dedication for him and all the others we lost." The two of them sat there most of the afternoon. Talking about all manner of things. Akio had given something the dream world thought they would never have. A new future.

Chapter 8

The End?

The next day, the whole of Danathor had gathered for the tribute to those who had fallen. Garron stepped up and addressed them.

"Today, you find yourselves in a world we never thought possible. Races, stand united, an ancient evil vanquished. But like with anything there comes sacrifice, hurt and death. Live full for those who brought us here. Teju, the man who prophesized the coming of the war. Raven, the first coming of a sign, which kept our hope alive for so many years. Michael, who may not have fallen, but created our world with all the power he had and laid the way for Akio. The boy from another world, who not only accepted a world thrust upon him, but gave all he could, so that we could live. We never really thanked him. So today I stand before you and say. Never forget him. Live for the chance you have been given." Up in the north watch tower, Norx noticed someone coming over the hill. He couldn't quite make out whom it was. Whoever it was seemed very injured and was barley walking at all.

"Sire! Someone approaches from the north!" He shouted to Garron interrupting the speech. Garron left the centre and joined Norx up in the north tower. The figure in the distance dropped down onto his front.

"Guardsmen, fetch the injured man and bring him in." Shouted Garron down to the north gate. They did as told and Norx and Garron watched as they ran out and over to the hill. They pulled up the man and supported him into the castle. Garron ran down to see who it was. He did not believe his eyes. By some kind of miracle, it was Akio.

"Bless my soul. Akio," Said Garron stunned. "How is this possible?" Yolanda heard Akio's name and rushed over. She flopped upon him, unbelievably happy to see him. Akio was barely conscious, still clutching at the sword of Michael.

"Take him to a room and soothe his wounds," said Garron to the guards. They nodded and took him into the castle. Yolanda went with them, not wanting to let go of Akio's hand.

Throughout the night and the next day, Yolanda never left Akio's side, every now and then dabbing his head with a wet cloth. Akio finally slowly opened his eyes. Yolanda smiled at him.

"You came back," she said sobbing.

"I said I would." Struggled Akio, smiling back at her. Yolanda hugged him so tight crying into his shoulder.

"How did you get back?" she asked. Akio started to sit up and propped himself up. He reached in his robes and pulled out the crystal.

"There beneath the destruction, I was stuck between life and death. But I saw a faint light and my heart would not let go." He put his hands on Yolanda's face. "I heard your voice Yolanda. Faint at first but it became clearer." Yolanda was listening intently.

"What did I say?" She asked.

"You said my name. You told me to hold on, and that I had to come back. Because you loved me." Yolanda smiled and welled up with joy. They hugged each other again and Akio lay back down. He did not yet have the strength to stand.

The next day Akio woke to find Yolanda asleep at the end of the bed. He softly got out of bed as not to wake her and picked up Michael's sword. He wandered down to the circular room and walked up to the plinth. He placed the sword back into the shield and stood back.

"Thank you Michael." He stood there for a moment and gave a thought to Teju, Tiny and Raven. He realized that the time was drawing near where he would have to go back to his world, although he didn't really know how. He then remembered that the map was in his pocket. He pulled it out and opened it up. As he did the final places appeared on the map and a train ticket fell out. He picked it up off the floor and read what it said. 'Home, one way.' He guessed it meant it was time. He had done what he came to do. He wandered back up to the room. The lighting woke Yolanda who sat up and saw the ticket.

"Not already?" she asked, upset. Akio sat next to her and held her hand.

"It seems today will be our last day together. Let's spend it well."

They spent the whole day together, walking through the gardens, taking a boat ride down the river and riding horses through the valley. Neither one wanted the day to end. But soon enough the sky began to dim and the sun began to set. A bright orange glow gleamed in the sky as the sun got lower. It was the most beautiful sight they had seen for a while. They made their way back to Danathor and were greeted by Garron.

"I guess the time has come, Akio. I suppose you'll be going back to the Skye city train station." Akio saddened at the thought of having to leave.

"Can we go with him, father?" asked Yolanda.

"Sure we can, if you don't mind transporting us back with you Akio?" said Garron.

"I don't mind at all, it would be nice," replied Akio taking both their hands. "Take a breath," he said to them. He then closed his eyes and transported them to Skye City. They appeared outside Mrs. Fritter's inn and Akio knocked on the door. She opened the door and was so pleased with what she saw.

"Akio!" she said grabbing hold of him for a hug. "You're alive. I'm so happy to see you. Mr. Yama." She shouted back into the house. Mr. Yama then appeared and saw Akio. His face lit up and he hurried forward. He rubbed his eyes thinking he was seeing things.

"You're alive."

"Come in, come in," said Mrs. Fritter moving aside. Akio then pulled out his train ticket and showed it to them.

"I'm afraid my time is up. But I couldn't leave without letting you know I was okay and saying goodbye." Mrs. Fritter and Mr. Yama became sad. They too had grown very fond of Akio and were so pleased to see him alive.

"I suppose the time had to come at some point. We'll come with you and see you off," said Mr. Yama grabbing his coat from a hook. Mrs. Fritter grabbed hers and they came outside and Mrs. Fritter shut the door behind her.

"There is just one place I would like to go first," said Akio. They made their way to where Tiny was buried and Akio knelt down and put a flower on the dirt. "I will never forget you Tiny. You saved my life and kept me company in lonely times. Sleep well, my little friend." He then stood up and set off with the others towards the station. When they arrived it was dark and the street and platform lights had turned on. Akio thought it was a shame the guard hadn't been at the gate, he would have liked to say goodbye. The train pulled up and hissed to a stop. He turned and took off his old sword and wand and gave them to Yolanda.

"Keep these for me. That way, I'll have a reason to come back." He took off his cloak and gave it to Mrs. Fritter. "Keep it clean for me, Mrs. Fritter." He pulled off his gauntlets and gave them to Garron. "You should find a use for these my friend." He then turned to Mr. Yama and went to give him the crystal.

"Keep it Akio. Then you will have a reason to remember us." Akio put the crystal back on and shook Mr. Yama's hand.

"I wouldn't forget you. Never," he said. He then turned to Yolanda and took her in his arms one last time. "This isn't goodbye, just farewell. I will always love you, no matter where I am. Every time you see a light in the sky. It will mean that I am thinking of you." He then tore himself away from her and stepped up onto the train and waved to them all. Yolanda held his sword and wand close to her heart and blew him a kiss. The door then closed and the train started off. He ran to the back window to catch one more glimpse of them and the world he had called home for the last year, but more so, the world that had taught him so much. It had showed him that even in the darkest of times, hope could always be found, as long as one had the strength to dream. The train then sped up and the city got smaller and smaller until it went out of sight. He sat down and let out a big sigh.

As the train went on, a strange thing happened. His clothes changed back into what he had been wearing the first day and he grew younger by a year. His hair shortened back to the length it had been and by the time the train had stopped at the other station, he was back to exactly the same. It was like it had all just been erased.

He got off the train and walked outside. The bus that had brought him here a year ago was waiting for him, so he wandered over and the doors opened. The hand from the driver's cab appeared pointing backwards with the sign on the window saying 'You know what to do'. He looked up at the destination wheel that spun round to say 'Home'. Akio then remembered and started digging into his pocket and he pulled out the map. He opened it up to take one last look, but it was not the same. It had shrunk down to its original size and was again completely blank. He huffed in disappointment handing it back to the driver before going down the bus and sitting down. The bus started off down the road. He already missed the dream world and the people from it a lot. But he had to return his mind to this world.

A couple of minutes later the bus came to a stop. Akio got up and walked down to the door. It hushed open and Akio got off. He waved to the bus driver, whose hand waved back. He was certainly home all right, the same bus stop he had gotten on a year ago. The bus then closed its doors and drove off down the road, disappearing when it reached the end. There was nothing left to do but walk home.

He made his way down the road and saw his house. He got to the house and opened the door and went in. His mum and dad were both sitting in the living room. He ran in and gave them both a big hug. It had been so long since he had seen them. For him anyway.

"Wow that's a big hug," said his mum. "If this is for slacking off all day and not helping with moving stuff in, I guess I can forgive you." She laughed. "Are you hungry?" Akio shook his head.

"Not at the moment mum," he said.

"So son, what did you do today?" Asked his dad. Akio sat on the sofa between his parents and smiled a big smile. He knew if he told them, they would never believe him.

The End

for Now..........................